THE ~~SLEEPOVER G~~ANG

Louise   Jo   Charlie   Alex

Louise is almost too terrified by her own story to tell it.

Alex can't wait to hear about the curse of the mummy's claw.

Jo is looking forward to spending the night in a haunted hotel.

Charlie is normally noisy and outgoing, but she's shy around a boy called Jesse . . .

The Haunted Hotel Sleepover

Sharon Siamon

**Hodder
Children's
Books**

a division of Hodder Headline plc

To Kate

Acknowledgements: The story that Louise tells in this book is a retelling of *The Monkey's Paw* by W. W. Jacobs, with elements from other great stories about wishes that came true, including *The Bottle Imp* by Robert Louis Stevenson and *The Fisherman and his Wife* from *Grimm's Household Tales*.

First published in Great Britain in 1997
by Hodder Children's Books

A CIP catalogue record for this title is available from the British Library

ISBN 0 340 67278 1

Typeset by Palimpsest Book Production Limited,
Polmont, Stirlingshire

Printed and bound in Great Britain by
Clays Ltd, St Ives plc

Hodder Children's Books
a division of Hodder Headline plc
338 Euston Road
London NW1 3BH

One

'Won't that elevator ever come?' Jo pushed the button again, and gave an impatient shrug of her slim shoulders

She and her three friends, Louise, Charlie and Alex, were waiting for the elevator in the small but elegant lobby of the Carleton Hotel in New York City.

'I wonder if the guys are on the same floor?' Charlie whispered, her dark eyes dancing.

There were two boys and four girls on this science expedition to the city. The boys were standing a little apart, with their teacher, Mr Makepeace.

'I heard that,' Mr Makepeace laughed. 'Yes, you're all on the fifth floor. You girls are in 521, the boys are in 507, and I'm in 430. I tried to get the rooms right together, but this was the best the hotel could do.'

The four girls glanced at each other and grinned. The further they were from Mr

1

Makepeace, the better. He had laid down firm rules – everyone was to stay in their rooms, and lights out at ten – but it was great that he wasn't on the same floor. Who knew what might happen tonight!

The four friends were so excited they could hardly breathe. 'I can't wait to see our room,' Louise said. 'I wonder if it will have a hot tub?' Her fair skin was flushed with excitement.

'No,' Alex laughed. 'This hotel was built long before hot tubs. Look at all this marble and carved wood, and this tiny elevator – here it comes at last!' Alex was tall and restless, with a mop of reddish blonde curls.

The elevator arrived with a gentle 'ding', and the door slowly creaked open.

Mr Makepeace, who was rather large, looked in and shook his head. 'We'll never fit in there with all our luggage,' he said. 'You girls go up with Mark and Jesse, and I'll wait for the next trip. Here are your room keys.' He jangled a handful of keys.

Jo, Charlie, Alex and Louise squeezed in with the two boys. Charlie kept her face turned towards the door, and the others saw a pink flush spread over her cheeks as the elevator slowly rose. Noisy, outgoing Charlie was shy where Jesse was concerned.

Jo tried to get a conversation going. 'What a weird old elevator,' she said. 'I heard a great story once about a ghost in an elevator,' she paused.

'Go ahead and tell us,' Alex's green eyes sparkled with amusement. 'We know you're going to, anyway.'

'Well,' Jo began, 'Some people were staying in an old hotel, just like this one. When they got on the elevator there was an old lady in a blue uniform, sitting on a stool in the corner. "What floor please," she asked in a sing-song voice, like she'd asked it a thousand times before.

'They told her their floor, but when her hand touched the elevator button they could see right through her skin! And then they realised the stool she was sitting on was floating, just above the floor.'

'A ghost elevator operator?' Mark scoffed.

'What happened next?' Louise shivered. She was easily spooked by the ghost stories Jo loved to tell.

Jo's voice sank to a thrilling whisper. 'The elevator got stuck, between floors. And when the hotel management finally opened the doors, they found the man and the woman stone cold dead, with looks of horror on their faces and their hair snow white.'

'You guys don't believe in that stuff, do you?' Jesse asked. He shoved his wire-rimmed glasses up on his nose.

'Jo does,' Alex laughed. 'She knows a million ghost stories.'

'Ghosts aren't very scientific . . .' Mark said.

'Maybe not,' Jo shook her head. 'But there hadn't been an elevator operator in that hotel for thirty years. And Mabel, the last to retire, was sometimes seen, sitting on her stool in the corner . . . right there!'

Just then the elevator gave a little shudder and stopped.

'Help! I want to get out of here!' Louise cried.

They waited, staring at each other. 'Jo, did you do this?' Alex shook a finger at Jo. She hated being shut in.

The elevator gave a groan, and started slowly up again.

'Phew,' Mark grinned, with a funny catch in his voice. 'I thought Jo's ghost was going to get us for a minute.'

'I'm sorry,' Jo laughed. 'But this hotel seems made for ghost stories.'

The door slid open and the six of them piled out. They were in a small lobby with many doors, and no windows. The light was dim.

All of them jumped when the elevator gave another 'ding' and creaked away towards the main floor.

'Spooky place,' Alex said. 'I'll bet it's a hundred years old.'

Charlie pushed open one of the doors. 'I wonder which way we go to get to our rooms?'

'They must be right down this hall,' Alex said. 'There's room 501.'

Two

Finding their rooms was harder than they thought. The Carleton Hotel was so old, and had been renovated so often, that doorways and halls branched in all directions. They dropped the boys off at their room and trudged on with their heavy bags. Finally, they stood in front of a solid-looking wooden door numbered 521.

'We should have left a trail of breadcrumbs,' Charlie groaned. 'We'll never find our way back to the guys' room.'

'Mr Makepeace would never have let us come up here by ourselves if he knew how weird these halls were,' Jo agreed.

'Anyway, we're here, at last,' Alex reminded her. 'Try the key, Jo.'

After a couple of tries, the key turned in the lock. The door swung in. The room was dark. Four ghostly figures stared at them from across the room.

'What's that!' Louise took a frightened step backwards.

Alex found the switch and the room flooded with light. 'It's just us, in the mirror,' she breathed.

The whole wall of the room opposite them was lined with mirrors.

There they were, reflected from head to toe – four girls in sweatshirts and jeans, gym shoes and sports socks. They'd spent the whole day setting up their science display for the state Science Fair. Tomorrow their projects would be judged in the finals.

'Look at us,' Charlie groaned. 'Our clothes are covered in salt, butter and school dust.' Their project was a solar-powered popcorn maker.

'Never mind! Check out this room!' Jo exclaimed. 'It's fantastic. Come on in and shut the door.'

They explored their private hideaway with glee.

'Two double beds and tons of pillows,' Alex exclaimed.

'Chocolates on our pillow!' Charlie cried, diving for the foil-wrapped discs tied with red ribbon. She was passionately fond of chocolate.

'No hot tub, but a whirlpool bath,' Louise

called from the bathroom. 'It's like a spa in here, and we have it all to ourselves!'

'Here's a whole little basket of soaps and shampoo, and a thing to polish our shoes . . . if we had shoes to polish.' Jo looked down at her grubby grey gym shoes and laughed.

'I wish,' Charlie suddenly said, 'I wish we'd brought nice clothes so we could go down to the hotel restaurant and order a fabulous dessert!'

'Picture us, sweeping into a posh New York restaurant,' Alex chuckled.

The four of them stared at themselves in the floor-length mirror. Their reflections stared back.

'I can't picture it,' Jo sighed. 'Not in these clothes.'

'Not in any clothes,' Charlie groaned. 'It wouldn't matter what I was wearing, I couldn't sweep across a floor like a super-model – not in a million years.'

'Let's face it,' Alex sighed, 'None of us could.'

'If you could change one thing about yourself, what would it be?' Jo asked, studying her own image in the mirror.

'I wish I was tall, like Alex,' Charlie burst out. 'I'm so short.'

'You might grow,' Louise said.

'Not me,' Charlie groaned. 'My mum is short, my dad is short, all my aunts and uncles are short. No wonder Jesse never notices me, I'm practically invisible.'

'Maybe he'd notice you, if you talked to him,' Jo said. 'He asked you twice about our solar project, and you just mumbled!' A quiet Charlie was a new experience for all of them. She was usually bursting with talk and jokes. But when Jesse was around she acted like a different person.

'Well, I wish I were skinny, like you, Charlie,' Louise sighed. She puffed out her round cheeks. 'I'd like to be able to eat a mountain of junk food, like you do, and not gain a gram.'

'What are *you* complaining about? I'd die for your blonde hair,' Jo said. 'Even your eyebrows are blonde.' She pulled back her own long dark hair and frowned at her reflection.

'Jo, you're crazy,' Alex shook her head. 'If I had one wish it would be to have your perfect nose and mouth.' She made a face at herself in the mirror. 'How would you like to have freckles, a crooked nose, a mouth too big . . . no wonder I love the circus. I look like a clown!'

'But at least you're tall!' Charlie bounced up on the bed and stared down at them in the mirror. 'Let's face it, if you took all our best points and stuck them together *we* would have the makings of a supermodel.'

'That's right,' Jo laughed. 'Take Alex's height, and Charlie's shape, and Louise's hair and my nose. We'd be a knockout!'

'I don't want to be perfect,' Charlie said. 'I just wish . . . if I could change one thing . . .'

Louise stared at the others in the mirror. 'That reminds me of something my great-uncle Taylor used to say: *Be careful what you wish for* . . . He told us this awful story about wishes that came true.'

'Hey! It's your turn to tell a sleepover story,' Jo whirled on Louise. The four friends got together whenever they could for sleepovers, and specialised in spooky stories, told late at night.

'Not this story,' Louise shuddered. 'I can't tell it. It was about a horrible ancient claw you wished on – something from an old Egyptian tomb.'

'Wasn't your Uncle Taylor an archaeologist?' Alex asked. 'Always away digging up old graves?'

'That's my famous great-uncle,' Louise nodded. 'But actually, a lot of the story happened here, in New York City.' She looked around the big, high-ceilinged room and shivered,

10

in an old building something like this.'

'You mean it's a true story?' Jo cried. 'This is perfect, Louise. You have to tell us!'

'Can't we just watch horror movies on TV, instead?' Louise asked.

'You hate horror movies,' Alex looked surprised. 'They scare the wits out of you.'

'They're not as bad as this story,' Louise shook her head. 'It frightened me so much as a kid that I've tried to forget it.'

'It sounds perfect,' Jo cackled. 'Let's pull the mattresses on the floor, and dim the lights . . .'

'Do you think the hotel would like that?'

'They'll never know. We'll put it all back in the morning.' Jo started yanking the heavy flowered bedspreads off the beds. 'Come on, it'll be fun . . .'

At that moment, the telephone rang. Startled by the sudden shrill beeps, Alex made a dive for the desk.

'Hi,' she said. 'Yes, we did. No, we won't. All right, we will.'

'Who was it?' Charlie cried. 'The guys?'

'No, it wasn't the guys. It was Mr Makepeace, reminding us that we are supposed to stay in our rooms and have the lights out by ten.'

'If he thinks we'll be asleep just because the lights are out, he doesn't know us,' Jo grinned.

Three

'I'm not a great storyteller, like Jo,' Louise said. 'But I can promise you'll never forget *this* story. Even when I think of that mummy's claw, I get shivers down my arms.'

'Wait, we have to get the atmosphere just right,' Jo jumped up and dimmed the light until the lamps were just a pale glow through their cream silk shades.

'Pull the curtains,' Charlie suggested. Neon light from the top of a nearby building flashed lurid red and yellow through the curtains.

'Nice! Weird! Very spooky,' Jo approved. 'Okay, Louise, you can start.'

'Ooo-h. I don't want to do this – I'll terrify myself.' Louise flopped on her stomach on one of the mattresses and pulled the hotel pillows under her chin. The light from the lamp over her head made her eyes look huge.

The others watched in a semi-circle. Jo lay flat on her stomach, her chin propped in her hands. Alex sat cross-legged, hugging a pillow. Charlie was on her side, leaning on one elbow.

The old hotel made funny noises as they waited for Louise to start the story. Doors banged down the hall, thumps echoed through the walls and sudden whines burst from the plumbing.

Louise's voice sounded hushed and frightened as she began to speak.

This story starts in Egypt, in the 1930s. My great-uncle Taylor heard it when he was digging for hidden tombs of the ancient Pharaohs near Luxor. Years before, another archaeologist had a horrible accident. The man's name was Dr Felix Sanger. A tomb that Dr Sanger was exploring caved in on him, crushing his skull. It took his team a whole day to dig Dr Sanger out, but they were afraid it was too late to save him.

Dr Sanger had a thirteen-year-old daughter, Alena, who was with him on the expedition. When he knew he was going to die, Dr Sanger called Alena to his bedside in the hospital in Luxor. He pressed a small carved box into her hand.

'It's the mummy's claw . . .' he whispered.

Alena thought her father's mind was wandering. She tried to pry open the small black box.

'No!' Dr Sanger cried. 'You must not open it. It has cost me my life and now I am afraid it will harm you, too.'

'What's in here?' Alena asked. She was very frightened that her father was so ill, but she had never really loved him. He had always been too busy chasing his own dreams to spend any time with her. Alena's mother had died when Alena was born, and she had been looked after by a long line of babysitters, nannies and tutors ever since. None of them stayed with Alena long enough to love her, and Alena could only clearly remember the last two or three in line.

Because of this strange upbringing, Alena was a stiff, cold person. She was proud of being able to look after herself, of keeping a firm grip on her feelings. Her father had married her mother because she reminded him of a statue of a Greek goddess, and Alena had the same straight nose and high cheek bones. Her hair was honey-coloured, and her eyes honey-brown, but there was no warmth in them.

She would be sorry if her father died. But

she couldn't say she'd miss him very much. Right now, she was filled with curiosity about the carved black box in her hand.

'What did you say was in here?' she asked again.

'It's a claw – the claw of a sacred bird – a falcon. It was preserved and entombed with the Pharoah to protect him in the afterlife.'

Alena wanted to tell her father to skip the history lesson. But she thought it would not be polite when he was so sick. Anyway, that's how he always talked – long, boring lectures about people who had been dusty and dead for thousands of years.

'I have not prepared for this moment,' she was astonished to hear him admit. 'I have nothing to leave you but your grandfather's legacy and this cursed claw – and this *you must not keep*. You must get my assistant, Farah, to help you take it back to the tomb where I was injured, and leave it there.'

'Why don't you just throw it away?' Alena asked.

'No!' Dr Sanger's voice was raspy and beads of sweat trickled down his face. 'Once you own it, you cannot throw it away. You must give it to someone else, and they must . . . accept the gift.' His voice sank.

A nurse came over with a worried frown.

'I'm afraid he's had enough,' she said to Alena in a low voice. 'You must go.'

'NO!' Dr Sanger tried to shout. 'If I die with this in my possession, it will harm her. I must tell her what to do!'

The nurse shook her head, and walked away.

'But how, father?' Alena asked. 'How can an old bird's claw harm me?' She was still looking for a way to open the box.

'Don't look at it,' he begged. He tried to grip Alena's arm, but his hand was too weak.

'When Farah brought it to me, I too thought it was a fake – something to sell to foolish tourists. Farah said it had magical powers. He said it would grant three wishes. Of course, I didn't believe him, but as a joke, I tested the claw's powers. I was desperate for money. My funds for the dig had almost run out. I wished for money – to carry on for just another year. I knew I was close to discovering the Pharaoh's tomb. All I needed was another fifty thousand dollars and I would be famous forever!' Dr Sanger groaned, and rolled his head from side to side.

'So, I wished on the mummy's claw, and the money arrived the next day. The news came in a telegram – my father had died, suddenly, of a heart attack, and left me exactly fifty thousand dollars. So I had my funding, but at a terrible cost – my father's life.'

A tear rolled out from under Dr Sanger's closed eyelid. This frightened Alena more than anything she had heard. She had never seen her father cry. As for her grandfather, she had never known him. She supposed it was sad that he was dead, but after all, he must have been old.

'I still didn't believe . . .' Her father was struggling to speak again. 'I thought it must have been a cruel coincidence – the money coming so soon after I had wished for it. But just to make sure, I wished to find the Pharaoh's tomb.'

Dr Sanger put his hand over his eyes. 'The claw struck with terrible speed. Yesterday, as I was walking through the Valley of the Kings, the earth suddenly opened and I fell down into the tomb. Part of the ceiling collapsed on me, and I woke up here . . . The claw likes to play terrible tricks. Before I passed out I saw that the tomb was empty, after all. No gold, no mummy – the grave robbers had been there before me . . .'

Alena looked at her father's bandaged

head. All she could think about was how foolish his long search had been – twenty years to find a tomb that Egyptian grave robbers had known about for thousands of years.

'And now,' Dr Sanger's voice was only a whisper. 'I have used my final wish – not for myself, but for you, Alena. I have wished for a safe haven for you in New York. Farah says wishes that are cursed are only the selfish wishes, the ones you wish for yourself. I hope he is right. If someone comes, offering to take you to New York, believe them, and go . . .' His voice drifted off.

The nurse came hurrying back. 'You really must go now,' she told Alena. 'Do you have someone to take you home?'

'No,' Alena said. 'I have no one, and I have no home. I'll wait outside, to see the doctor.'

She got up and walked out of the hospital room, the small box clutched in her hand.

There were chairs against the wall of the corridor, and Alena sat down, arranging her skirt carefully around her.

Then she opened the box.

*   *   *

Louise paused. She brushed back her blonde hair.

'What was in the black box?' Jo shrieked. 'For heaven's sake, Lou, don't stop there!'

'We know it was the claw,' Alex said. 'But what did it look like?'

'Are you . . . are you sure you want me to go on?' Louise's voice quavered. 'I'm not doing a very good job of this.'

'YES!' her friends chorused.

'This is a great story,' Jo gave a shudder. 'I feel so sorry for Alena's father.'

'I don't think I like Alena,' Alex said. 'I mean, I know she's been neglected, but not everybody would turn out to be such a cold fish when their father was dying.'

'She sounds cool, and perfect,' Charlie sighed. 'I'll bet she was tall, too.'

Just then there was a knock on the door. The girls turned shocked faces to each other.

'Who's that?' Jo whispered. 'Should we answer it?'

'We'd better get these mattresses off the floor, first,' Alex whispered back. 'It might be somebody from the hotel.'

'Or a serial killer,' Charlie whispered cheerfully. 'This *is* New York.'

There was a frantic flurry as the four girls

19

tried to heave the two heavy mattresses back on the beds. They were much easier to slide off than put back.

The knocking continued. A steady THUMP! THUMP! THUMP! on the wooden door.

Four

'Girls? Are you in there?'

'It sounds like old Makepeace,' Alex whispered fiercely. 'We'd better open the door.'

Jo undid the bolt and opened the door a crack, leaving the chain in place.

'Mr Makepeace?' Jo asked, trying to peer through the crack.

'You got that right!' It was Mr Makepeace's favourite expression. 'I just came to make sure you were settled in.'

Jo flipped off the chain and opened the door. 'We're fine,' she nodded. 'See?'

Mr Makepeace looked shocked at the heaps of blankets and pillows piled on the mattresses on the floor. 'Well . . . I see you've . . . made yourselves at home,' he stammered.

'It's science, Mr Makepeace,' Charlie shot in. 'We're investigating . . .'

'Making sure there are no bugs in the bedding,' Jo added quickly. 'But if there *are* bugs we're going to capture them and study them – wildlife in a New York hotel!'

Mr Makepeace's broad face broke into a beam of joy. 'The scientific spirit. How wonderful,' he cried. 'Let me know if you find anything. Wonderful. We'll be meeting at the elevator at eight sharp tomorrow morning,' he went on. 'I've arranged a wake-up call for your room, and for the boys. Have a good sleep now. Tomorrow's a big day!'

The door banged shut and the four of them collapsed in giggles on the floor. *'Bugs in the bedding,'* Charlie gasped. 'Nice work, Jo.'

'I hope there aren't really any bugs . . .' Louise peered nervously at the heaps of bedding.

'If there are, we'll just stay up all night and study them,' Alex chortled. 'It will be another of our famous projects: BEDBUGS AND THE WHIRLPOOL BATH.'

No one in their home town of Lakeview would ever forget the science project that had brought the sleepover gang together. They had built an engine that ran on smelly methane gas – which was fine until the methane exploded in the school gym. Now they were working on using the sun as an energy source. It smelled better.

'How about BUG POWER?' Charlie suggested. 'We could harness hundreds of cockroaches to run on treadmills and produce electricity.'

'*You got that right!*' Alex did a perfect imitation of Mr Makepeace. '*Wonderful!*'

'Ugh! Stop!' Louise put her hands over her ears. 'I'll be feeling cockroaches crawling over me all night.'

'Yes, stop,' Jo agreed. 'Otherwise Louise will never get back to her story, and we'll never find out what happened when Alena opened the box.'

'I'll go on,' Louise said. 'But can we just not talk about bugs scuttling around in the dark? Please!'

'All right, but it's just so easy to tease you,' Charlie's eyes sparkled. 'I'm sorry, Louise, go on.'

They settled themselves among the heaps of blankets and pillows, eager for Louise to pick up the story where she had left off.

Louise shivered. There was a look of fear and disgust on her face as she spoke in a halting voice.

Alena sat back with a gasp. She stared at the open box on her lap, resisting the urge to sweep it to the floor, to get up and run. A smell of death and decay seemed to rise from the box.

The box was black and lined with red silk. Resting on it was a dried and shrivelled foot of a bird. Three wrinkled toes were outstretched, the fourth was curled horribly under. Each ended in a cruel, yellowed talon. The part where the bird's foot had been severed from the leg was tipped with gold.

Alena's head swam. Through the dizzy haze a white figure swayed before her. Two arms reached out towards her. Alena gave a cry and snapped the box shut. Immediately the haze cleared, and there, standing in front of her in his long, flowing, Egyptian clothes, was Farah, her father's best friend and head of the excavation team.

'Alena . . . I am so sorry. The doctor has just spoken to me. Your father is gone.'

Alena rose to her feet. 'You mean, he's dead,' she said.

Her head was still swimming, but she was very calm.

'He was a good man. I am sorry.' Farah stood very straight in his long white djellaba. His head was bowed.

'He asked me to tell you something,' Alena said.

'What?' Farah raised sorrowful eyes.

'He wanted you to take this back to the tomb . . .' Alena opened her hands, showing Farah the black box.

She was amazed to see Farah shrink back, trembling with fear.

'The mummy's claw?' His voice shook with terror. 'Is it in that box?'

'Yes,' Alena said. 'Do you want to see it?'

'No!' Farah cried, taking a step backward. 'Don't look at the claw. There is much evil in it.'

'If it is so evil,' Alena looked coldly at the man who was supposed to be her father's friend, 'why did you give it to him?'

'I didn't know,' Farah bowed his head again. 'An old man in ragged clothes brought it to me one night. He said to give it to the one who was searching for the Pharaoh's grave. He said it would bring good luck, grant wishes.'

Alena thought Farah was not telling the whole truth. But it didn't matter now. The important thing was to obey her father's dying wish.

She needed Farah's help to do this. All

of the other scientists working on the dig would think the claw was a precious relic from a tomb. They would probably bundle it up and send it to a museum somewhere. Maybe that would be better, but she had promised . . .

She looked hard at Farah. 'Tonight, after dark, you must come and take me to the tomb where my father died. We will leave the claw there.'

Farah shook his head, 'No!' He looked terrified.

'Yes,' whispered Alena fiercely. The doctor was coming down the hall towards them. 'Eight o'clock. Don't forget!' Alena hissed.

'Very well. I will come,' Farah muttered, and wheeled away.

In the next few hours Alena discovered just what a nuisance she had become. Everyone was very sorry, but no one knew what to do with her. She had no family, no friends, even her tutor had left at the end of the school term, two weeks before.

The ferry boat took them from Luxor, back across the Nile to the expedition camp near the Valley of the Kings.

While her father's co-workers discussed what to do with her, Alena waited in their tent. She pulled books out of her father's trunks, searching for clues to the mummy's claw. It seemed the most important bird in ancient Egypt was the falcon. She found drawings of the Egyptian god Horus, who had a falcon's head. Horus protected the Pharaoh, and was the god of the Sun. But he had a more menacing side, too. His father, Osiris, was god of the underworld. Now she understood why people believed that the falcon protected the king after death, as well as when he was alive.

After an hour had passed, Dr Butterworth, the head of the expedition, bustled into the tent.

'Alena, my dear,' he said nervously. 'I see you are bearing up bravely. No tears, eh? Good girl.' He rubbed his hands together. 'We have been quite puzzled about what to do, as you can imagine. Your father left no will, no instructions. But in the last half hour we have been so fortunate – it is almost as though fate has taken a hand in our hour of need.'

'What are you talking about?' Alena said. She disliked the way Dr Butterworth fussed and flapped his hands.

'Why, my dear, someone has come. A Mrs Van Dorf, on the tour boat from Cairo. She

27

is a distant relative of one of the students working on the dig. When she heard of our difficulty, she instantly volunteered to take you back with her to New York. Isn't that splendid?'

Alena remembered her father's words. If someone comes, you must trust in the power of the claw and go with them. And now, this person had appeared.

'But where will she take me in New York?' Alena asked. Her father had asked for a safe haven for her in that city.

'She says she knows of a wonderful residence for young women.' Dr Butterworth babbled on. 'Come. I want you to meet her. You will love her.'

It was so obvious that he was desperate to get rid of her that Alena wanted to kick him. But she rose stiffly to her feet and followed him to the small building that served as expedition headquarters. She had no other choice.

She did *not* love Mrs Van Dorf. The woman wore a close-fitting turban on her head, and a long, droopy suit. She looked like a rich, boring tourist. And worst of all, when she talked, she gushed.

'My poor, poor, darling girl,' she said,

as she dived at Alena, smothering her with perfume and pearls. 'Of *course* you must travel with me. We will have such an *enchanting* time.'

She wanted to take Alena back to her hotel in Luxor that very moment.

Thinking of Farah, and the mummy's claw, Alena said firmly that she would be happy to go the next morning, but she must have time to sort out her father's things.

'But alone, in a tent?' Mrs Van Dorf looked unhappy. 'This is no position for a girl of your age.'

'I will be fine,' Alena said, pressing her lips together. She prided herself on her ability to be on her own, and often wondered why other people always needed to be with someone else.

The sun went down in the desert like a red hot stone dropped behind the hills surrounding the Valley of the Kings.

Alena waited to hear Farah's footsteps crunch on the gravel outside the tent.

Sharp at eight, he appeared.

The night was cold. Alena followed Farah's swishing white robe along the dark paths. The valley was honeycombed with tombs of the dead Pharaohs of Egypt. Some of them, like the tomb of King Tut, were famous. Others were forgotten, or undiscovered.

'Here.' Farah stopped at last. 'This is the tomb.'

'Are you sure?' Alena asked. It was impossible in the dark to see where they were.

'Yes. Be careful. It is this part that collapsed when your father was inside.'

Alena knelt down in the dark desert night on the edge of the tomb, seeing her father's face as she had last glimpsed it, begging her to return the mummy's claw. Her father's mind must have been affected by his injury. It was so unlike him to believe in something as unscientific as magic.

Alena wasn't sure she believed any of this nonsense about wishes and evil powers attached to a dried-up old bird's foot, either. But terrible things had happened to Howard Carter and Lord Carnarvon, who had discovered King Tutankhamen's tomb, just a few hundred metres away, and many people believed in the curse of King Tut's tomb.

The desert night seemed to close around her, like a shroud.

Farah struck a match to light one of his thin Egyptian cigarettes. 'Be quick,' he hissed.

Alena drew back her hand. 'Light another match,' she whispered. 'I want to throw it as far back in the tunnel as I can.'

The match flickered in the cavernous darkness. Alena threw the small box containing the mummy's claw with all her strength into the hollow depths of the tomb.

The mummy's claw was gone.

'Don't you think it's weird,' Alex said. 'This story is about the sun god's power in ancient Egypt. And *we're* using the sun's power in our science project. I wonder what the old Egyptians would think of our popcorn maker?'

'I don't believe in magic,' Charlie sighed. 'but I wish there *was* such a thing as three wishes. I'd wish to be tall, and for a lifetime's supply of chocolate, and . . .' She stopped.

'And Jesse Smith,' Jo laughed. 'You wish he'd walk up and say "I've always liked you, Charlie, but I've been too shy to tell you."'

Five

'I wish you guys would quit teasing,' Charlie groaned. 'Let's just get back to the story and forget about boys.'

'What happened to Alena after she threw the claw into the tomb?' Alex asked. 'She had such an adventurous life – travelling around the world, living in expedition tents – I can't help envying her.'

'Mrs Van Dorf tried to dress her in the latest fashions,' Louise said. 'She took Alena to Paris and bought her a fancy steamer-trunk full of new clothes in the latest 1930s' style.'

'Wait!' Jo cried. 'Start where you left off. I want to hear all the details.'

'I can't remember everything,' Louise wailed. 'I'm sure I'm leaving out all the best parts.'

'No, you're not,' Charlie said. 'This is the best story I've ever heard. Good old mummy magic – no werewolves, no ghosts . . .'

'Well,' shuddered Louise, 'not yet.'

They all flopped on their pillows and mattresses again. 'This is as exotic as a Sultan's tent in the desert,' Jo sighed.

Louise coughed, cleared her throat and went on in a shaky voice that got stronger as she spoke.

Three weeks later, after their stopover in Paris, Alena was on a ship, heading for New York City with Mrs Van Dorf.

It was a luxury liner, and Mrs Van Dorf travelled first class. There was dancing every night and elegant meals at the Captain's table.

Alena spent most evenings by herself, wearing one of the formal dresses Mrs Van Dorf had bought for her, watching Mrs Van Dorf twirl around the floor with one of her many partners. No one asked her to dance, and Alena thought she would die of boredom before the boat docked in New York.

It was a great relief when the weather turned stormy in the middle of the Atlantic and most of the passengers got seasick. Mrs Van Dorf took to her cabin, and Alena was free to prowl the decks, watching the towering waves rise and fall, listening to the screaming of the wind.

She was not sick. Her appetite was excellent. She ate almost alone in the huge dining salon. On the third night of the storm, a monster wave tipped the ship almost on its end. All the expensive china and crystal went sliding down Alena's table to crash to the floor. Alena held on to her plate and glass and calmly went on with her dinner.

But afterwards, in her cabin, she discovered that the force of the wave had knocked over her trunk. It was a large steamer-trunk with gold corners, hangers on one side, and rows of little drawers on the other. Now the contents of the drawers were spilled across the cabin floor.

With a sigh of annoyance, Alena set the trunk back up on its end and started gathering up her belongings.

Suddenly she stopped short, her feet riveted to the floor. There, in the centre of the clutter, was a small black box.

'No!' Alena breathed. She felt her head swim as it had on the day her father died.

She crossed the floor in a daze, reached down for the box and forced herself to open the lid.

The ugly shrivelled claw lay on its bed of crumpled silk. It must have been in one of the drawers of the steamer trunk. But how had it got here – in the middle of the Atlantic?

Farah! Alena thought furiously. Somehow, he must have climbed into the crumbling tomb and found the claw in its box. Then he had smuggled it into her trunk.

Well, she had had enough of the mummy's claw. Wrapping herself in a raincoat, Alena grabbed the small black box and ran from the cabin, up to the ship's deck.

The night was a torrent of wind and waves. Lightning flashed as the ship heaved and twisted through mountainous seas. The wind blew foam from the tops of the waves into Alena's streaming face.

If she tried to throw the claw into the wind on this side of the ship, it would fly right back at her.

She fought her way to the other side, grasping at the railings to keep herself from sliding down the wet, heaving deck.

'Now!' she cried. 'Goodbye, you ugly thing!' She hurled the claw with all her force into the teeth of the storm, letting the box skitter away overboard, into the ocean.

Then she turned and ran – right into the arms of one of the crew, who caught her and held her tight.

'Miss!' he bellowed. 'What are you doing out here! You must come in . . . look!' He pointed behind her. 'Even the sea birds can't fly in this wind.'

Alena turned and saw, beating its powerful wings, a huge brown and white bird with outstretched talons.

'They follow the ship's wake,' the sailor shouted an explanation, as he drew her into the shelter of an upper deck. 'They pick up garbage we throw overboard, and in a storm like this we give them protection from the worst of the weather.'

Alena shuddered. She had seen no bird out there before. Not until she threw the claw into the air. Now the bird swooped and called hoarsely, then vanished.

'Strange,' the sailor muttered as they watched it go. 'I've never seen a sea bird that looked like that.'

It *must* be a sea bird, Alena thought in terror. But, for a second, it had looked like Horus, the falcon, the ancient sun god of Egypt.

Louise stopped talking and cleared her

throat. 'I need a drink of water,' she croaked. 'I'm not used to talking so long.'

She jumped off the mattress and ran into the bathroom.

The others sat in silence, listening to her run water in the sink.

'The claw is following her,' Jo gasped. 'Her father *said* she couldn't throw it away. He gave it to her – she had to give it to someone else.'

'Or, maybe she was right,' Alex shook her head soberly. 'Maybe Farah sneaked back into the tomb, got the claw, and hid it in her trunk. It's possible.'

'What about the bird?' Jo asked. 'It must have looked so spooky, suddenly appearing out of the mist!'

'Just a coincidence,' Charlie laughed. 'I don't believe in all that curse stuff. Now the wishes – that's another thing.'

'I wish this water was cold!' Louise sputtered, coming back from the bathroom. 'Yuck! It tastes like bath water.'

'That's a wish I can make come true!' Charlie bounced off the mattress and grabbed the ice bucket on the desk. 'I saw an ice machine near the elevator. Let's go!'

'But Mr Makepeace said . . .' Louise began.

'He said we were to stay put. He didn't say we should die of thirst.' Charlie's eyes sparkled.

'And we have to keep our storyteller in top form,' added Jo.

'*You got that right*,' Alex did her Mr Makepeace imitation. 'This is the best sleepover story we've ever had, Louise. We have to keep you going.'

'I don't know,' Louise shivered. 'It gets pretty terrible. I'm not sure I can tell it . . .'

'You're doing a wonderful job so far . . .' Jo patted her friend on the shoulder. 'Come on. Expedition Ice Machine is on its way.'

Six

Their route down the dim hotel hallway took them past the boys' room, 507. Charlie tiptoed to the door and pressed her ear against the wood.

'These darn thick doors,' she whispered. 'I can't hear Jesse, or Mark. Wait a minute . . . I hear someone laughing.' She turned to the others and made a face. 'They're watching TV. I should have known.'

'How typical,' Jo snorted. 'Here they are in this fabulous old hotel and all they can do is sit in front of the television, exactly like they do at home.'

'We'll have to think of a way to liven up their evening,' Alex agreed. 'Like this – get ready to run!'

Alex pounded on the boys' door with all her might and the four of them took off down the hall at top speed.

'Through here!' Jo gasped as they hurtled through a fire door and down a flight of corkscrew stairs with an elaborate iron-work railing.

'Neat old stairs,' Charlie panted. 'But does anybody have any idea where they go? This hotel is like a maze!'

'We must be on the fourth floor, or maybe even the third,' Jo said, pushing open a door.

'Listen,' Louise cried. 'I hear an ice machine.'

The big metal cabinet was just around the corner. Alex held it open while Charlie scooped enough ice cubes to fill their bucket. It was so silent in the depths of the hotel that even the ice cubes clattering into the bucket set their teeth on edge.

Louise popped a smooth small cube in her mouth. 'This tastes a lot better than the tap water,' she sighed.

'Let's go back up the stairs,' Jo suggested. 'We'll never find our way to the elevator from here.'

The quiet of the hotel hallway was almost spooky, the stairs totally deserted.

'I'll bet no one has used this spiral stair-case since Mabel was an elevator operator,' Charlie panted. 'It looks a hundred years old.'

'Probably tons of ghosts in an old place

like this,' Jo said, opening the door at the top. 'Think of all the people who die in hotels – heart attacks, murders . . .'

'Let's not,' shivered Louise. 'Is the boys' door shut?'

They paused in front of it, hearing the roar of the TV. 'They probably didn't even hear me knock,' Alex said in disgust. 'Should I do it again?'

'No, they might think we're just trying to get their attention,' Jo stopped Alex's hand. 'Let's think of a better way to annoy them, later.'

There were nods of agreement. The four girls tiptoed past the boys' door, and found their way back to their own room.

'Have a nice long drink,' Jo told Louise, when they were all inside. 'I want to hear what happened when Alena got to New York.'

'That is, if the ship didn't go down in a hurricane,' Alex said.

'No,' Louise shook her head with a shudder. 'The ship made it safely right here to New York, just the way Alena's father had wished.' Louise tossed back her blonde hair. 'Of course, there was a twist.'

The four of them settled down once more on

the heap of hotel mattresses. They propped themselves up on luxurious pillows and expensive bedspreads. Neon light filtered through the curtains and flickered across Louise's face as she began to speak.

Two days after Alena threw the mummy's claw into the ocean, the ship sailed into New York Harbour. Alena watched for the landmarks she remembered – the Statue of Liberty and Battery Park at the tip of Manhattan Island.

It was a chill October day. Alena had forgotten the cold autumns in this huge city. As the ship slid into its berth, she saw that almost everyone on the crowded dock was wearing a hat and coat. She shivered in the damp wind that came up off the water.

Taxis were lined up two deep along the docks. In the 1930s there were no passenger flights across the ocean, so everyone who came to America arrived by boat.

Mrs Van Dorf hailed a cab. 'We'll go straight to Haven House,' Mrs Van Dorf told Alena. 'Miss Calvert is expecting us.' She gave the address to the taxi driver and they zoomed off into the streaming traffic.

As the taxi sped towards Park Avenue, Alena felt how fast the whole city seemed to move. The windows of the department stores beckoned with expensive shoes, dresses and jewels.

Mrs Van Dorf gushed on about Victoria Calvert, the woman who ran Haven House. 'She is accepted in *all* the best circles,' Mrs Van Dorf said. 'I've known her for simply *years*. Her father and mother, bless them, started this home for orphan girls and Victoria has carried on their wonderful work. She is a *treasure*, my dear.'

The taxi pulled up in front of a narrow brownstone building, where a flight of stone steps led up to the front doors. Over the doors, etched in limestone, was the name, *Haven House, 1903*.

Something about the name sent shivers through Alena. A safe haven was what her father had wished for. The name, Haven House, seemed almost a cruel joke.

'Of course, there aren't so many orphans these days as in old Mr Calvert's time,' Mrs Van Dorf babbled on. 'Oh! Sorry my dear, I forgot. You are an orphan yourself, now. Well . . .' she adjusted her turban, paid the taxi driver and tugged Alena out into the street.

'One of the *best* neighbourhoods,' she gushed. 'This used to be an elegant hotel in the old days. I'm sure you will be happy here.'

It was at this moment that Alena realised she was about to be abandoned to total strangers. A feeling of panic paralysed her for a moment. It was not that she'd ever had close friends or relatives, except her father, but even the people on the expedition, even Mrs Van Dorf, however annoying, had known who she was. Now she was about to be cut adrift in an old New York hotel, taken charge of by people who didn't know her from a hole in the ground.

Alena straightened her already straight shoulders and marched up the steps behind Mrs Van Dorf. She was ready.

Inside Haven House, her eyes took a minute to adjust to the dim light. After living in a tent under the hot Egyptian sun, after the sunlit cabin of the ocean liner, Haven House felt like a tomb. Alena's courage deserted her. She felt like running back through the doors, out of this place.

Almost no light filtered through the small panes of the front doors into the entrance lobby. There was a carved wooden counter at one side, and double sliding doors on the other side, tightly shut. Straight ahead was a narrow hall and an ancient elevator cage.

Mrs Van Dorf nodded impatiently to the maid who had answered the door. 'Tell Miss Calvert that Daphne Van Dorf is here,' she snapped.

The maid dipped her head and hurried away down the hall. Did she seem frightened, Alena wondered, or was it just that she couldn't see her face clearly? Why on earth was it so dark in the gloomy hall? It must only be four o'clock, and already it seemed like night in this house.

She heard a door close at the end of the hall and approaching footsteps. A black hotel cat scurried out of the way.

Once more, Alena felt a sense of panic, an urge to run back on to the busy New York street and take her chances there.

Too late. Victoria Calvert had seized her hand and was peering sharply into her face with enormous hooded eyes on either side of a beaklike nose.

The woman's mouth looked small and cruel. She was gorgeously dressed in some flowing, form-fitting dress, with a fluttery, feathery shawl fastened with a diamond clip around her shoulders. Her short, carefully waved hair fitted her skull like a cap.

'Alena? What a charming name.' She swirled around Alena. 'Ever since I got Daphne's wire I've been dying to meet you. So sorry to hear about your father, but you're in safe hands here. Rose will take you up to your room.' She pointed to the young maid. 'Now, Daphne, my dear, come into the parlour. We must talk.'

She swept Mrs Van Dorf away through the double sliding doors, leaving Alena and the maid in the hall.

'This way, Miss,' Rose led the way to the elevator cage. 'Miss Calvert said you were to leave your bag here. Someone will bring it up.'

'I can carry it,' Alena said. She had packed her most precious possessions in a small overnight bag. Some instinct warned her not to let it out of her grip.

The elevator creaked up to the third floor. From there, a narrow flight of stairs led to a fourth floor. Rose opened a door with a key. The room was small and mean, with one tall, grimy window and ugly beige walls. Against one wall was crammed a narrow metal bed.

Alena caught her breath in amazement. She had had more space in the desert tent.

'This will be your room,' Rose said.

'But what about the rest of the house?' Alena gasped. 'There must be larger bedrooms.'

'Oh, yes, Miss,' Rose nodded. 'But Miss Calvert said you was to sleep here.'

'Where are all the other girls?' Alena asked.

'Some's at school, some's at work,' Rose looked sad. 'Some work here, in the house, like me.'

So Rose was an orphan too. 'All right,' Alena nodded, anxious to be rid of Rose. 'Thank you.'

She waited until Rose had clattered down the narrow stairway, and then quietly followed. She watched Rose hurry past the elevator cage and open a door further along the third floor hall.

Alena followed, finding the doorway led to a spiral staircase, leading down. It was like looking down a dark well. She saw Rose's white cap disappear through a door far below. Alena had got used to stairs like this on the ship. She slipped quietly down, and made her way to the first floor to listen at the closed parlour doors.

As she had suspected, they were talking about her.

'There is almost a hundred thousand dollars altogether,' Mrs Van Dorf was saying. 'The girl has money from her grandfather, as well as insurance from the university which employed her father.'

'A nice sum,' she heard Miss Calvert murmur. Then there were some words she couldn't catch and then, 'Of course you will have your usual finder's fee, Daphne.'

'And I've earned it,' Daphne Van Dorf sighed. 'The girl is a perfect horror – so cold, so rude.'

Miss Calvert laughed unpleasantly. 'All thirteen-year-old girls are horrors, my dear, as you well know. I hope all the legal and financial papers are in order?'

'I did my best,' Mrs Van Dorf sniffed. 'You have joint guardianship until she is eighteen.'

'*Joint*?' Alena, listening, could just see Miss Calvert's arched eyebrows rise. 'Joint guardianship with whom?'

'With old Dr Butterworth, who is usually on the other side of the world, digging up bones. I'm sure you can get around him, Victoria. He had no interest in the girl, or her money. When she is eighteen, the residue of the estate goes to Alena, of course.'

'Of course,' Miss Calvert laughed again.

'Only, of course, there will be nothing left, as usual.'

'So expensive,' Mrs Van Dorf murmured. 'School, clothes, food . . .'

'It's work I do from the goodness of my heart,' Miss Calvert replied.

Alena had heard enough. Now she knew what she was up against at Haven House. An unscrupulous woman who stole the inheritances of helpless girls!

She fled back up the dark spiral staircase to her room, and flung herself down on her creaking bed.

The mattress was like a board. Something was jabbing into her shoulder. Alena turned over restlessly, reaching under her body to remove the sharp object.

She sat up with a horrified start. Her hand had touched something hard and sharp and wrinkled. It seemed to burn her hand.

Throwing back the bedspread, Alena covered her mouth to shut off a scream of terror. It was the claw, the claw she had hurled into the storm, the mummified falcon's claw tipped in gold.

Alena stared at it in shock, her thoughts whirling. 'How? When?' she cried. Perhaps it was all part of the plot to get her money. Someone had planted a claw in her trunk,

49

another in her private bag to frighten her, to make her lose her mind.

Her bag still lay on the bed. 'Someone could have gone through it while I was downstairs listening at the door, and hidden the claw under the bedclothes,' she whispered to herself. Her eyes searched the little room, as though looking for the person who had done this to her.

But, even as she did so, Alena was haunted by her father's words: *You cannot throw it away*. She had tried twice; once at the tomb, and once flinging the claw into the ocean, and here it was, back again.

Seven

Alena heard thunder rumble over the city. She ran to the small window at the end of the room. The window looked out over a forest of rooftops, and beyond those towering skyscrapers, shutting out the sky.

Alena found herself trembling. This place was like a prison – the dark, dreary city closing in around her, the storm making the high small room a place of shadows.

She turned back, quaking, to her bed where the claw lay, staring up at her, its twisted talons ugly and yellow-grey. She couldn't stand to look at it!

Alena fumbled through her bag and found a blue velvet pouch that she used to keep her jewellery safe. She dumped the necklaces and brooches Mrs Van Dorf had bought her into her bag, Then, carefully, not really wanting to touch the horrible thing, she put the claw in the pouch and pulled the drawstring tight.

She took a deep breath and backed away from the pouch lying on her bed. It was as if the claw was calling to her: *Use me to escape this place – make a wish.* Alena ran from the room, down the stairs to the third floor.

Here the hall was wider, the doors further apart.

She stood, uncertainly, wondering what to do, where to go.

A pale, quavering light, close to the floor, seemed to beckon her down the hall. It moved slowly, and had no definite shape. The hotel cat streaked past, its fur standing on end. As Alena got closer, the light disappeared.

Now the sound of sobbing drew her further down the hall. There were brass numbers on the dark wooden doors, another hold-over from the days when Haven House had been a hotel.

Finally, she found herself outside the room where the crying seemed to be coming from. Something made her reach out and rap on the door.

'Who's there?' came a wrenching, heartbroken voice.

'Alena Sanger. I'm a new girl,' Alena said.

There was silence behind the brown door.

Alena thought whoever was inside must not want to be disturbed. She was turning to go when the door burst open and she was face to face with someone from a movie screen, or a dream.

Even with tears running down her cheeks, smudged eye makeup and rumpled blonde curls, the girl was lovely. But that was not what made her so striking. It was the way she held the door, the slender grace of her arm, the angle of her head. She seemed five or six years older than Alena, and seemed totally different to anyone she had ever met.

'Hello,' she said. 'Come in . . . I'm Tracey Winters.'

Alena entered the dingy room, and Tracey shut the door behind them. It was a bit larger than her own room, with a window that overlooked the street, not the back of the building.

'I suppose Miss Calvert has stuck you up on the fourth floor,' Tracey said. 'Poor lamb, and in this storm, too.'

Her voice was low, and full of pity. Alena had never been spoken to that way. She gulped, then burst out with a question. 'Why were you crying? I heard you all the way from the landing.'

'Oh dear. I hoped the thunder might mask my wailing,' Tracey collapsed on her bed. 'The truth is, my life is a ruin.'

The way she said *ruin* sounded like sea waves in a cave. She raised tragic blue-grey eyes to Alena.

'It is?' Alena asked, curious how anyone so extraordinary could be in trouble.

'An *absolute* ruin,' Tracey said, burying her face in her hands. 'Everything I've dreamed of is slipping away. Everything I've wanted for so long.'

She stood up and began to pace the narrow room. 'And now Ben wants me to marry him and leave it all behind. He says it's my only choice – to go home and leave all this forever.'

The thunder crashed again as she spoke, and Tracey threw herself face down on her pillow.

Alena had seen illustrations of grief-stricken princesses in books that didn't look half as beautiful as Tracey, flung across her bed, her tear-stained face buried in the crook of her arm.

'But why wouldn't you want to leave this awful place?' Alena stammered. 'Don't you, don't you love Ben?'

'LOVE HIM?' Tracey sat up suddenly

and threw out her arms. 'Of *course* I love him. I adore him. But he wants me to be his *wife*!'

'And that's so terrible?' Alena was now bursting with curiosity.

'He wants me to give up my dreams of being a great actress, a great star,' Tracey said in mournful tones. 'Oh, I suppose it's hopeless anyway, but I wanted it so much.'

She turned her blue-grey eyes to Alena. 'I honestly don't know if I can live if I can't be on the stage.'

Alena let out a long breath. So that was it. Tracey was an actress. No wonder she looked and sounded like a movie star.

'But . . . you're so lovely,' she stammered. 'I don't understand why you can't . . .'

'Because no one will give me a chance,' Tracey cried. 'Just one chance to show them what I can do. But I can't get through the door, I can't even get an audition so someone can see me, or hear me.'

'There must be a way,' Alena said. If ever anyone looked like they belonged on the stage it was Tracey Winters. Her energy seemed to fill the small room at Haven House, putting even the thunderstorm to shame.

'I've tried everything,' Tracey said despairingly. 'And now I'm out of money. Miss Calvert won't let me stay a moment longer than I can pay the rent for this miserable room.'

After what she had heard downstairs, Alena was sure Tracey was right. There was no charity in Victoria Calvert.

'You can see, can't you, why I just can't be an ordinary wife?' Her eyes were large and appealing. Light seemed to shine from her so that Alena had a hard time not to stare.

'Yes, I can see,' Alena murmured. She tried to picture this girl standing at a sink or a stove stirring soup, and the picture that came was of Tracey with tears pouring down her cheeks.

'. . . To wish for something all your life, to come so close, and then fail,' Tracey sobbed.

Alena heard echoes in her mind. Where had she heard this kind of talk before? But the echoes were drowned by the flood of admiration she felt for this girl.

'But you poor darling,' Tracey dashed the tears from her eyes. 'You've just arrived and you're listening to all this rubbish. Where did you come from?'

'Egypt,' Alena answered.

To her astonishment, Tracey rose up and

danced around the room, her face transformed with excitement.

'EGYPT!' she cried. 'Just to hear that word! Just to imagine . . . Are you, could you be, Egyptian?'

'No,' Alena said, almost bowled over by the sudden change in this amazing young woman. 'I'm American. My mother was Greek.'

'That explains your wonderful eyes. But you've been living in Egypt. How marvellous! Where? Near the pyramids? Near the Sphinx?'

'No,' Alena shook her head. 'In a tent, in the Valley of the Kings. My father was an archaeologist searching for the tombs of the Pharaohs.'

'Stop! You must tell me all the details – this is just too amazing.' Tracey's eyes were on fire. Somehow, Alena knew, she was not just being gushy. She really cared.

'Do you . . . are you interested in Egyptian tombs?' she asked.

'Oh, darling girl. When I see pictures of the treasures of Tutankhamen, I feel I must have been part of that world in another life. I played Cleopatra in *Antony and Cleopatra* at school. It captured my soul. And you, you have *really* been there.'

Alena could only nod.

Tracey swept around the room, arms out-stretched. 'O how lucky, lucky, *lucky* I am that you were sent to me! But why on earth did you leave Egypt?' She plunked back down on the bed and stared into Alena's eyes. Her gaze was so intense that Alena almost had to look away, but she found herself telling the whole story of how she had ended up at Haven House.

For the first time in her life, Alena felt truly wanted and important. It was a new sensation. Tracey was really interested in her!

By the end of Alena's story, Tracey had clasped both her hands in her own long slim ones, and looked as though she was going to start crying again.

'If only I had met you earlier! But now I must pack and get ready to leave New York.' Tracey wore again her look of tragic despair. 'It's the end of all my dreams. My rent is paid just until the end of this month.'

'I can help you,' Alena said. 'I have lots of money.'

Louise paused and reached for another drink.

'Haven House isn't much of a safe haven,' Charlie grumbled.

'Imagine that Calvert woman taking all Alena's money,' Alex shook her head.

'Yes, and a hundred thousand dollars was a lot more money back then,' Louise nodded. 'Great-uncle Taylor said it would be worth almost a million dollars now.'

'And the mummy's claw is back,' Jo shivered. 'Why does it keep turning up?'

'I wonder if it's true that someone is trying to frighten Alena by putting duplicate claws in her luggage?' Alex asked. 'She must have been ready to jump out of that fourth floor window when she felt it under her shoulder – ugh!'

'Alena's cool. I guess the thing about being cool is that you stay cool in a tough situation,' Charlie said. 'But I would have freaked if that thing turned up in my stuff *again*.'

'I warned you it was a ghoulish story,' Louise said. 'It gives me the creeps to think of it, and it gets worse.'

'It's making me ravenous,' Charlie cried. 'I have to get something to eat.'

'See,' Louise groaned. 'You're always hungry, always eating, and you stay as thin as a stick.'

'How can you be ravenous,' Jo said. 'We just had a hamburger, fries and a milkshake each before we came up here.'

'Fast food,' Charlie shrugged. 'It goes through me fast. I need something solid for dessert.'

'Well, if you're serious,' Jo said, 'why don't we call room service?' She flourished a large fancy menu. 'I found this in the desk drawer. Listen: *dark chocolate double fudge mousse cake*. Or how about *double cherry cheesecake with chocolate shavings*?'

'Stop! Yum – you're driving me crazy,' Charlie groaned. 'How do we get this stuff?'

'We just call up and order and it comes to the door,' Jo explained. 'We don't have to get dressed up and go down to the restaurant.'

'Then let's do it,' Charlie danced around the room. 'Quick, before I starve to death.'

'You phone, Alex,' Louise suggested. 'Do your imitation of Mr Makepeace's voice.'

Eight

Twenty minutes later, the food arrived. Jo answered the knock at the door. A young bellboy wheeled in a cart covered with white linen and four silver domes. He looked a little startled at the bedding on the floor.

'Here you are, ladies,' he said, with a grin, removing the domes one by one with a flourish.

'Double cherry cheesecake . . .

'Deep dish key lime pie . . .

'Chocolate mousse cake . . .

'Triple fudge sundae with nuts, cherry and Grand Marnier . . . Are you sure you can eat all this?' he grinned.

'We're sure,' Charlie nodded.

'Where do I sign?' Jo asked, trying to sound as adult as possible.

'Right here. Your name and room number,' the bellboy whipped a card out of his clean white jacket pocket.

61

Jo signed her name with a flourish and Alex handed the bellboy a tip.

'Enjoy yourselves,' he grinned again and slipped away, shutting the door.

'Ooo-h, I'm in heaven,' Charlie sighed as she dived into her triple fudge sundae.

For a few minutes there was only the sound of slurps and sighs and clicking spoons as the four desserts rapidly disappeared.

'I could eat *ten* of those,' Charlie beamed, contentedly.

'I wonder what the food was like at Haven House?' Alex said, licking her lips. 'Tell us, Louise.'

Louise shuddered. 'The food was one of the worst things,' she said.

'Keep going with the story,' Jo begged. 'Now that Charlie's ever-empty stomach is full.'

'It's not full,' Charlie corrected her, 'but it's happy. Go on, Louise.'

They lay back happily on the mattresses as Louise settled herself on the pillows. A frown of concentration creased her forehead as she took them back to Haven House, and to Alena's struggles. There was anger and indignation in her voice as she started to speak.

*　　*　　*

Alena was used to eating strange foods from around the world. She had eaten sheep's eyes in Morocco, raw fish in Japan, and ground raw lamb in the Middle East. But even though she might not like it, there had always been enough food, wherever she and her father travelled.

At Haven House things were different.

As Alena and Tracey were talking, a gong sounded from the depths of the house. Tracey leapt to her feet.

'Dinner. Hurry!'

'But I want to talk to Miss Calvert about helping you pay your rent,' Alena cried. She had never had such an unselfish thought in her life – had never wanted to help someone else. Now that she had the idea of helping Tracey, she didn't want to let it go.

'Later,' Tracey grasped her hand. 'If we don't hurry, there'll be nothing left!'

There was a look of such desperation on her face that Alena shrugged and let herself be dragged along – out the door, down the hall, into the creaking elevator and along another hall to the dining room.

The light in the dining room was as dim as the rest of the house.

Through the gloom, Alena saw two long tables with two rows of bent figures fiercely buttering thin slices of bread. Small glasses of milk stood at each place.

Alena and Tracey slid into their places and Tracey murmured hello to the girls around her as she reached for two slices of bread from the plate in the centre of the table. The pile was going down fast.

'One at a time,' someone muttered with her mouth full.

'This is for *Alena*,' Tracey said grandly, making Alena sound like some kind of goddess. 'She's not used to how fast we have to eat around here.'

A bell tinkled at the end of the room. Alena saw Miss Calvert's fluttery blue shawl in the dim light.

'Good evening girls,' Miss Calvert cried. 'As you know, there has been a storm. Unfortunately, it has cut off power to the kitchen, so there will be no hot meal tonight.'

There were groans and sighs from the two rows of seated girls, but no one challenged this ridiculous statement.

'But the lights are on in the rest of the house,' Alena said loudly. 'How can that be possible?'

There was an awful silence. Alena saw thirty hostile eyes drilling into her.

'Hush!' The girl next to Alena dug her in

the ribs with her elbow. 'Shut up, or we'll get no dinner at all!'

'It was a freak of nature,' Miss Calvert swooped over to Alena and hovered behind her chair. 'Girls, this is Alena Sanger. She's new here. I'm sure you will give her a true Haven House welcome.'

She gripped Alena's shoulders with both hands, and Alena could feel her sharp fingernails ready to dig in. 'I'd like to see you in the parlour after dinner,' she murmured. 'You and I need to have a little chat.'

'Yes, I want to talk to you, too.' Alena said, very clearly. She was not going to let this horrible woman frighten her.

'Don't let her know we're friends,' Tracey whispered, as Miss Calvert fluttered away with a piercing glance back over her shoulder.

'Why not?' Alena said in surprise.

'Because she'll make sure we never see each other until I'm out of here,' Tracey said.

'Why do you all let her treat you this way?' Alena whispered back. 'There can't be anything wrong with the stove. We have to have more than bread and milk for dinner!'

'Can't you shut up?' the girl who had poked her with an elbow hissed.

'Alena, this is Marion,' Tracey introduced them. Marion had curly brown hair and a long, lean figure.

'Marion's a dancer,' Tracey said.

'Yeah,' Marion laughed loudly. 'These days I stay on my toes in ladies' wear at Macy's Department Store.'

'Alena's from Egypt,' Tracey said. 'She just arrived in New York.'

'Yeah? Well, welcome to Calvert's haven for lost souls, honey!' Marion shrugged. 'Say, are you going to drink that milk or just look at it?'

'You can have it,' Alena said quickly. 'I've got to go – Miss Calvert's motioning me to come.'

'Good luck, honey,' Marion whispered. 'Don't let her make you cry.'

'And don't forget,' Tracey murmured as Alena stood up, 'we don't know each other.'

It was amazing, Alena thought, as she made her way between the rows of bent heads, how Miss Calvert had made all these people terrified of her. Some of them looked her own age, but many of them were almost grown-up, like Marion and Tracey.

As soon as she entered the dimly lit parlour, Alena blurted out, 'I'd like five hundred dollars of my money. There are clothes I'll need for school, and I have nothing warm for winter.'

'Five hundred dollars is a great sum of money,' Miss Calvert was perched behind her elegant desk. She had changed to go out for the evening, and wore a deep red dress, cut low in the back and in a V at the front. 'We will see you get everything you need.'

'But I want my money,' Alena insisted. 'I'm old enough to shop for myself. I've been doing it since I was ten. You have no right to keep my money.'

'Of course, we'll make sure you have pocket money,' Miss Calvert went on as if Alena hadn't said anything. 'Five dollars a week should be more than enough.'

'And another thing,' Alena took another step towards the desk and glared at Miss Calvert. 'I want a larger room. I'm used to more space.'

'I'm sure all that can be arranged,' Miss Calvert said smoothly, 'just as soon as the bank clears your money.' She gave Alena a cruel glance. 'Until then, you are here as a charity girl, at my own expense, and the charity girls sleep on the fourth floor.'

Alena was stunned. 'How dare you . . .' she spluttered.

Miss Calvert got up from behind her desk and draped a bony bare arm around Alena's shoulder. Alena would have twitched away, but she was aware of the long fingernails, ready to clutch.

'I know you've had a difficult time, and a long journey,' Miss Calvert said in a low, powerful purr. 'But you really can't speak to me like this, you know. I *am* your legal guardian.'

'With Dr B-Butterworth,' Alena stammered.

'Yes, of course, dear Dr Butterworth, so far away in Egypt, at the moment. I'm sure he would agree that someone must take charge of you . . .' There was a slight dig of the fingernails. 'Whatever you think, you are far too young to have control of your own money, or make decisions about your daily life.' Another dig.

'Luckily,' Miss Calvert glared down at Alena with her hooded eyes, 'I am prepared to take on the responsibility.' She sighed. 'Young girls like yourself are at a difficult stage in life. Fortunately, I have had a lot of experience. *I know how to deal with girls like you.*' Her eyes glittered like the diamond and ruby clip in the centre of her dress. 'I'm late for my dinner engagement,' she said harshly. 'I'm sure you can find your way back to the fourth floor.'

She swept out of the room, leaving Alena shaking with helpless rage.

Alena met Tracey in the elevator. 'Did she tear a strip off your hide?' Tracey asked.

'No. But I can't believe she's really got all of my money,' Alena blustered. 'I wanted to pay your rent for another month, and she won't let me have *any* of it!'

'I knew that's how it would be,' Tracey looked sorrowful. 'But at least we'll have a couple of weeks together. You can tell me all about Egypt, and who knows? Maybe something will turn up for me at the last minute.'

The elevator had reached the third floor.

'Do you want me to come to your room now?' Alena asked as the doors opened.

'I promised to meet Ben,' Tracey apologized. 'He'll be waiting for me, down on the street. He always whistles *Yankee Doodle* so I know he's there. But we'll bring you back something better than bread and milk. Meet me at my door at nine-thirty.'

Alena nodded. She ran to the hall window to look out. Three floors below, she could just make out a tall figure in the light from the street lamp. The faint strains of a whistled tune came floating up. Then Alena saw Tracey tripping down the steps of Haven House and linking arms with the tall young man. They walked away, down the wet, glistening sidewalk.

Alena climbed the last flight of stairs to her room. She steeled herself to take the pouch containing the claw and bury it at the bottom of her bag. Then she kicked the bag under the bed and flopped down on to the hard mattress.

She lay there, watching the storm play itself out in the tiny square of sky she could see from her window.

It seemed an agony of time until nine-thirty came. Alena had been lying on her bed in her clothes. She got up quietly and tiptoed to the door.

She was glad she had explored the third floor hall while it was still light. Miss Calvert clearly liked to save money on electricity. Now it was very dark, and she had to feel along the wall to guide her.

Suddenly, she saw that same, strange blue light, making it possible to see the numbers on the doors. But when Alena reached 42 it blinked out, leaving her in the dark. She was aware of some *presence* in the darkness, almost as if another person were close by.

The cat shot through her legs with a yowl of terror. Feeling panicked, Alena banged too hard on Tracey's door.

'Hush!' Tracey opened the door and drew her in. 'Whatever you do, don't let old Calvert hear you!'

Tracey had been to the diner on the corner. 'Here's a sandwich, and some pudding for dessert,' she said, spreading her riches out on the small bedside table.

'You shouldn't have spent your money,' Alena cried.

'But, my poor darling, it's your first night, and everything must seem so strange,' Tracey said.

Alena nodded. 'It is the strangest place I've ever lived,' she agreed. 'What's that funny blue light I keep seeing in the hall?'

To her surprise, Tracey looked like she might faint. 'So, you've seen her already,' she gasped. 'You *are* a remarkable girl.'

'Seen who?' Alena stared.

'People say there's a ghost in this house,' Tracey said in her low, dramatic voice, 'but not everyone can see her. I never have. They say she was an orphan, in the time of Miss Calvert's father. She died here and she haunts the halls, always cleaning, crouched by the floor.'

'The cat can see her,' Alena shivered, feeling her own hair standing on end. 'How did she die?'

'There were rumours that the Calverts murdered girls and buried them in the rose garden,' Tracey sighed, 'but nothing was ever proved. It's rather like the story of the frog in the boiling water.'

Alena looked puzzled.

'They say,' Tracey explained, 'that if you put a live frog into a pot of boiling water it will try like crazy to jump out of the pot. But if you put a frog in a pot of cold water and then raise the temperature one degree at a time, it will just die without a struggle. I think Polly, the poor orphan who died, just perished slowly of loneliness, overwork and poor food.'

'But the Calverts killed her all the same,' Alena cried, standing up straight and throwing back her head. 'Well, I'm going to be like the frog that's been thrown into the boiling water. I'm going to fight until I get out!'

'Good for you,' Tracey smiled. 'But don't be afraid of Polly's ghost. She's never harmed anyone, that I know of. It's Miss Calvert you need to watch out for!'

How strange, Alena thought, as she climbed back to the fourth floor, that her father would wish her a safe place to live, and she would fall into the clutches of a greedy woman like Victoria Calvert, in a haunted hotel.

'Can it *really* be the mummy's claw at work?' she asked herself out loud. She had been raised to think like a scientist. Curses and magic powers were not scientific.

And yet her father had believed in the claw's powers at the end.

Alena shuddered. She had tried to throw the claw away and it had come back twice. She had hidden it in her bag, shoved it under her bed. What should she do with the claw now? Leave it in her luggage and wait for a chance to offer it to a museum or a collector of ancient Egyptian artefacts?

Whatever happened, Alena thought, she must find a way to keep Tracey at Haven House. Otherwise, she would really feel unsafe.

Nine

In the next few days, Alena discovered how Miss Calvert kept the girls at Haven House in a state of nervous terror.

First, there was the constant hunger. When Alena went down to breakfast the next morning, she heard grumbling and angry whispers.

'No orange juice,' Tracey groaned.

'Yeah,' Marion stood with her hand on her hip. 'Rose says the orange juice is gone for good. It's prune juice from now on.'

'But why?' Tracey said. 'We all like orange juice. Nobody will drink prune juice!'

'That's the whole point,' Marion said. 'We were drinking the orange juice too fast. It was costing Witch Calvert too much money.'

'But that's so stupid,' Alena cried. 'She saves money by buying food nobody eats?'

'Sh-sh,' Tracey hushed. 'Things will be worse if you complain.'

'I don't see how they could get worse,' Alena grumbled.

She was soon to find out that they could. For dinner there was disgusting bread pudding made out of breakfast toast crusts. For lunch, there was watery soup made from last night's leftovers.

Then there were the idiotic rules. Everyone had to be up at six, and in bed with the lights out at ten. No visitors, except in the parlour. No male visitors, at all. Tracey had to meet Ben outside, and if she was late, the doors were locked and she was left on the street. The girls were closed in, cut off from the life of the city around them except for school or work.

As if that were not bad enough, there was the constant spying at Haven House. Somehow, Victoria Calvert knew everything about the girls under her roof. No one had any secrets. Alena found that out the second day, when Miss Calvert called her into the parlour.

'I don't think Tracey Winters is a good companion for you,' Miss Calvert said. She was dressed this morning in an expensive dark suit, with a fox fur collar. The two fox heads glared at Alena with their glass eyes.

Alena gaped at Miss Calvert, speechless.

'I have my ways of knowing these things,' she went on. 'You admire her tremendously, and she is attractive, but Tracey is just a cheap little nobody from Wisconsin, and *much* too old to be a friend for you.' She gave Alena a superior smile, pursing up her narrow lips.

'It's none of your business . . .' Alena stammered, '. . . who I choose as a friend.'

Victoria Calvert's smile hardened into a fierce glare. 'That's exactly the kind of tone I will not tolerate from you,' she hissed. 'I don't think I need to say more. You will find me a helpful friend, but a very terrible enemy if you go on testing me in this way. I have already asked Marion to leave.'

'Marion's gone?' Alena gasped. 'Why?'

'I found out . . . certain things about her,' Miss Calvert said. 'And I never liked her attitude.'

Miss Calvert raised her hooded eyes to Alena's. 'There's one more thing. There's no use being secretive about your person, or your belongings. Hiding things under your bed, for example. Put your possessions in your drawers or closet . . . and do not sleep in your underwear in this house. It's unsanitary. Rose will provide you with nightgowns which you may also keep in your drawers.'

Alena burned with fury and shame. How did she know what she wore to bed? How *dare* she snoop through her private things? What if she had found the mummy's claw?

And, finally, there was school. Miss Calvert had lost no time enrolling Alena in the least expensive and most rigid school in New York City. The uniforms were long, grey wool tunics, worn over stiff white shirts. The grey stockings were thick and itchy, the shoes heavy. After her light, loose expedition clothes, Alena felt like she was in a strait jacket.

Six other girls from Haven House trudged the dreary, wind-swept streets to the grimy school building. None of them tried to make friends with Alena, and she did not care. They were all dull and stupid, she thought, probably from spending their lives at Mr Burns' school!

Alena hated sitting, hour after hour, copying pages from big encyclopaedias. She had learned most of what Mr Burns taught them years ago. Alena had previously enjoyed arguing with her tutors, but the slightest word of disagreement here brought a crack on the knuckles with a ruler from Mr Burns.

Alena could feel herself slipping backwards. She felt as if she was turning as grey as the city around her. Between hunger and the dark October weather and the packed tight streets of New York, she could feel her desire to struggle weakening.

This was nothing compared to what was happening to Tracey. They met secretly every night, whispering so that Miss Calvert and her spies couldn't overhear. 'I can't hold out any longer,' Tracey told Alena at the end of the week. 'I have to give Miss Calvert notice that next week will be my last.'

'I've written to Dr Butterworth,' Alena cried. 'I'm sure when he knows what's happening, he'll help me get some money.'

'But it could be weeks until he answers,' Tracey gave Alena a warm hug. 'I love you for trying to help, but it's no use.'

'Won't Ben give you some money?' Alena asked. 'He's supposed to be in love with you.'

'Oh, he loves me,' Tracey said. 'He followed me here from Wisconsin, and he's been trying to look after me, but he doesn't think I'll ever make it as an actress. He says if I were really any good, I'd be discovered by now. He thinks . . .' tears shone in Tracey's eyes, 'he thinks it's all in my head, this wanting to be a star on Broadway, and the sooner I get over it and go home to Wisconsin and marry him, the better.'

'But it's not true,' Alena protested. 'I *know* you can be great. You mustn't give up!'

'I'm trying to get an audition for the chorus line in a new musical at the Majestic,' Tracey smiled through her tears. 'They've called an open audition – that means anyone can try out. I'll give it one more shot tomorrow. In the meantime, I'll have to give old Calvert my notice. Don't worry, if I get the part, we'll move out together.'

Alena felt a surge of happiness. Wouldn't that be wonderful – to live with Tracey! She looked with wonder at her beautiful friend. Why couldn't everyone see how marvellous Tracey was? How thrilling she would be on stage? Every day on her way to school Alena passed the theatres with the names of the stars in lights. Tracey's name should be up there!

'Good luck with your audition,' she whispered as she said goodnight.

Tracey put her finger to her lips. 'Actors are very superstitious,' she warned. 'In the theatre it's bad luck to say "good luck". Say "break a leg" instead.'

Alena laughed. 'All right. Break a leg tomorrow.'

The next day was cold and rainy. On top of her hated school uniform, Alena had to wear a woollen coat and hat. The wind whistling up the canyons of the tall buildings cut through all those layers as though laughing at her puny efforts to keep warm. 'You were meant to be cold today,' it seemed to say, 'and nothing can change that.'

When Alena staggered up the stairs of Haven House that night she wondered about Tracey's audition. Had she got a part?

But later, when she sneaked down to Tracey's room, she found her friend with a pale face, packing her things.

'What happened?' Alena cried.

'I stood all morning in the rain, outside the theatre,' Tracey said in her tragic voice. 'By the time I got on stage, I was so cold I could hardly croak. They listened to two bars of my singing and waved me off the stage. They didn't even say "thanks", just "NEXT!" It was *so* humiliating!' She buried her face in her hands. 'Ben's right. I'm no good. I can't even get a part in the chorus.'

'You didn't have a fair chance,' Alena said.

80

'It's the only chance I'm going to get,' Tracey said. 'And there's worse. Look at this.' She handed Alena a crumpled, tear-stained piece of paper.

It was a bill. Alena read it and looked up in surprise. 'What does this mean?'

'It says I owe Miss Calvert fifty dollars – for *services*!' Tracey's voice was bitter. 'If I can't pay, and I *can't*, I can work it off in the kitchen.'

'I don't *believe* this!' Alena was shocked.

'You can believe it. Most of the servants here were "guests" at one time. Their money ran out and they had nowhere to go.'

'Like poor Polly,' Alena gasped.

'Yes, I'm sure that's what happened to her, too. I have to get out of this room tonight, and start cooking breakfast at dawn tomorrow.'

'Are you going to do it?' Alena was aghast.

'Yes, I'm going to do it. I don't want to start married life with Ben in debt to him for fifty dollars.'

Alena could see Tracey's mind was made up. Her face was a mask of determination and despair.

'Tell me about Egypt, to cheer me up

while I pack,' Tracey said. 'Tell me something to make me forget my problems.'

'Well, there's the mummy's claw . . .' Alena faltered. Without being quite sure why, she began to tell the whole story of the claw, and how her father had wished on it. 'I don't, I *can't*, really believe in it,' she finished, 'but in a twisted way his last wish came true.'

'Oh, what a pity you threw the mummy's claw into the ocean!' Tracey cried. Her face was alive with excitement.

'Well, yes and no,' Alena stammered. 'It's come back, you see.'

'What do you mean?'

'It was on the bed when I arrived. It must have been in my hand luggage, I suppose. Maybe I only dreamed I threw it away in the storm.' Alena knew she wasn't making sense, but Tracey didn't seem to care. Her eyes were sparkling.

'Of course! The claw is following you, because you own it. You can't throw it away. You have to use the wishes.'

Alena gaped at her. 'Haven't you been listening? If you believe in the power of the claw, then it killed my father!'

The rain had begun to beat on the window again.

'But he was looking for the Pharaoh's tomb. The falcon god protects the Pharaoh in the afterlife. You told me that yourself.'

'So?' Alena was beginning to be frightened by the eager light in Tracey's eyes.

'*So*, if you wished for *other* things, not related to the Pharaoh, the wishes might not be cursed,' Tracey cried.

'That's what my father thought,' Alena said. 'He wished for a safe haven for me in New York.'

'Well, you got here, didn't you? And you're safe, at least until your money runs out. And you met me!' Tracey said excitedly.

That was true, Alena thought. Meeting Tracey was the best thing that had ever happened to her.

'Maybe you were meant to help me,' Tracey sat on the bed and gripped Alena's hands tight. 'Could I . . . could I see the claw?'

Now Alena was really frightened. Once more, the look in Tracey's eyes reminded her of someone.

'Please,' Tracey begged. 'I just want to see if it's still where you left it.'

'Oh, no!' Alex said. 'Don't tell me Tracey's going to wish on the claw.'

'It's Alena who has the three wishes,' Charlie pointed out, 'not Tracey.'

'She would never use them,' Jo shuddered. 'Not after what happened to her father.'

'But she'd do anything for Tracey,' Alex pointed out. 'She worships her.'

'Louise! Don't keep us in suspense. Tell us what happened!'

'Don't you want a drink, or something . . . to wash down that gooey dessert?' Louise asked. 'I could sure use one.'

'I saw a vending machine in the lobby downstairs,' Charlie nodded. 'Let's go.'

'I think Louise is just putting off telling us what happened,' Alex chuckled. 'It must be something *awful*.'

Ten

The four girls retraced their steps down the dimly lit hallway. Near the elevator they passed a glassed-in fire hose set into the wall.

'Stop!' came a spooky voice from behind. 'GO NO FURTHER.'

They stopped and turned in amazement.

'LOOK!' Louise screamed.

The door to the fire hose compartment was slowly opening.

'What *is* going on?' Alex shouted.

The hose began to snake outwards, its brass nozzle twisting from side to side like the head of an alien reptile.

The Sleepover Gang found themselves backing up, almost tripping over each other.

'It's reaching out for us. It's alive!' Louise shrieked.

'Listen,' Jo cried. 'It's saying something.'

'I AM THE HAUNTED FIRE HOSE,' the low voice bellowed. 'YOU ARE SUPPOSED

85

TO BE IN YOUR ROOM. YOU ARE NOT SUPPOSED TO BE PROWLING THE HALL.'

'Wait a minute,' Charlie whispered. 'How does it know we're supposed to be in our room?'

'THE HAUNTED FIRE HOSE KNOWS ALL!' the voice growled.

'I smell a rat!' Alex raced forward and grabbed the fire hose.

'WAIT,' the hose boomed. 'I'M HERE TO WARN YOU. YOU MUST NOT USE THE ELEVATOR. YOU MUST OBEY YOUR TEACHER.'

'Two rats . . . named Mark and Jesse,' Jo breathed a sigh of relief. 'Wow! How did they do it?'

'Remote control robotics. It's their science project. Remember?' Alex said in disgust. 'They've probably been out here all night figuring out how to make us look stupid . . .'

'By rigging up the fire hose to act like a snake,' Charlie agreed.

'They were counting on us using the elevator,' Jo said. 'Look, there's the trip wire that starts the door to the hose compartment opening.' She pointed to a fine wire stretched across the floor.

'But how did they make it talk?'

'Here's Jesse's tape recorder,' Charlie held up a mini-recorder. 'It's probably programmed to start when the fire hose door opens.'

Alex shook her head. 'But how would they know it was us? What if someone else used the elevator?'

Jo's dark-blue eyes scanned the elevator lobby. 'You can bet they are somewhere around here,' she muttered.

Just then they heard muffled snorts of laughter behind the fire door to their right. Jo wrenched it open. There were Jesse and Mark rolling on the floor, helpless with laughter. Surrounding them was a clutter of remote-control equipment.

'Nice trick!' Alex said.

'We'll get even,' Jo promised.

'You should have seen your faces,' Mark roared. 'Ooo-h – the haunted fire hose!'

Charlie punched the elevator button for the ground floor.

'We're going to get pop from the vending machine,' Louise said. 'You guys want anything?'

'We've already been, four times,' Jesse said. He was red in the face from laughing. 'This robotics is thirsty work.'

* * *

A few minutes later, cans of cola in hand, the sleepover gang was back in their room. 'We'll have to think of something truly wicked to get even,' Alex groaned. She took a long pull on her straw. 'You know, the guys probably weren't even in their room when we heard the TV and banged on the door.'

'And we didn't see them at the elevator because we took the stairs to the ice machine,' Jo added.

'We should have *known* they were up to something,' Charlie said. 'Those guys are robot fanatics. Dangerous science dweebs. I can't believe I ever wanted Jesse to notice me!'

'That's right, forget him!' Jo bounced up and turned down the lamps again. 'I want to hear what happened to Alena and Tracey. Come on Louise, sit here.' She patted a spot for Louise to sit.

'Was the mummy's claw still in Alena's little blue pouch when they went to look for it?' Alex asked, snuggling down with her head resting on her elbow.

Charlie flopped down beside them. 'No more stopping until we find out if Alena made a wish on the claw,' she announced.

*   *   *

Louise tossed back her hair and stared at her friends. Her eyes shone in the faint glow of the lamps as her quavering voice began the story again.

The claw was in the velvet pouch where Alena had left it. She felt a sense of dread as she lifted it from the drawer, and, holding it by the drawstring, went back down the stairs to Tracey's room. The satin cords seemed to twist in her hand as if they were alive.

'It's in here,' she handed the bag to Tracey. 'Just look – don't take it out, *please*.'

But Tracey gasped when she looked in the pouch and dropped it in the centre of her bed. One talon of the claw stuck out of the opening.

'Shake it back in,' Alena whispered in terror. 'I hate the look of the thing.'

Tracey's face was once again alive with wonder. 'It came all the way from Egypt,' she cried in her low, dramatic whisper. 'All the way from a Pharaoh's tomb to help me. Alena, I *have* to look at it.'

She picked up the end of the pouch, gave it a shake and the mummy's claw, shrivelled and ugly, spun out on her white bedspread.

Alena's face was as white as the bed covering. 'It's evil!' she insisted. 'I wish I could get rid of it.'

'No . . .' Tracey shook her blonde head. 'It's very old, and powerful, but I believe it, *and you*, were sent to help me. You must wish on it for me, Alena. Wish that I become a Broadway star!'

Her eyes were shining like stars. Alena knew now where she had seen that look before. It was when her father talked about discovering a tomb full of treasure – a tomb that would make him rich, and famous forever.

Alena stared at Tracey. 'You can be a star without magic.'

'Maybe I'm not good enough,' Tracey said. 'Maybe I'm *not* better than all the hundreds of other girls who try out. But I *want* it more. I want to act and sing and dance in front of an audience so badly, I can't breathe without it. Alena, help me!'

She turned her imploring sea-grey eyes on Alena.

Alena felt the room spinning around. The mummy's claw seemed almost alive, lying on the bed. It was as if she could see Horus, the hawk-god, hovering over the room, waiting to swoop on Tracey.

'No!' she choked. 'It's all stupid make-believe. It's all old superstition. *I won't do it.*'

'Please,' Tracey begged again. 'It doesn't matter if you believe . . . *I* believe. Please, for me!'

Alena could hear her father's dying voice. *If the wish is for someone else, it will not be cursed.* It was almost the last thing he had said to her. He had been a scientist – and he had believed.

'All right,' she heard herself say, a sob in her voice for the father she suddenly missed with all her heart. 'All right. I wish on the mummy's claw that Tracey Winters becomes a great star.' She forced herself to pick up the wrinkled thing and hold it in her palm.

Was it only her imagination, or at that moment did the claw seem to spread its talons and dig into her flesh?

Alena seized it with the trembling fingers of her other hand and thrust it back into the pouch. 'That's it!' she whispered hoarsely. 'Whatever happens – no more wishes.'

The next morning, Alena crept down five flights of stairs to the kitchen, in the basement of the old brownstone hotel.

There was Tracey in an apron, standing at the stove, stirring thick, gloopy porridge. Tears rolled down her cheeks and dripped into the pot, but she made no sound. She looked so much like Alena's mental image of Tracey as Ben's wife that Alena stood frozen in the doorway for a second before stepping forward to squeeze her friend's arm.

'I'm sorry,' she said. 'I didn't think the wish would work.'

'I can't bear this,' Tracey sobbed. 'It *has* to work.'

At that moment, Miss Calvert stuck her head in the kitchen door. She was wearing a pearl-grey satin morning gown and slippers.

She frowned when she saw Alena and Tracey with their heads close together. 'This is no place for *you*, Alena Sanger,' she barked. 'Go and get ready for school at once.'

She whirled into the kitchen to face Tracey. 'As for you, you have had a telephone call. I explained that you were working as my kitchen maid, and took the number.'

She handed a slip of paper to Tracey who looked at the note and shook her head in puzzlement.

'He didn't leave a name, or message,' Miss Calvert said sharply. 'You know I don't tolerate men calling or visiting my girls. You may tell him that when you call back – *after* your breakfast duties are done.'

'Yes, ma'am,' Tracey said meekly.

Alena could see two spots of colour burning in Tracey's cheeks. Alena thought they were spots of fury, but Tracey was burning with excitement, not anger.

'Stir this for me,' she cried, as soon as Victoria Calvert had swished from the room. She thrust her wooden spoon into Alena's hand. 'I'm going out to the diner on the corner and calling this number!'

Clutching the slip of paper in her hand, Tracey dashed out the servants' entrance without even taking off her apron. Alena could hear her footsteps running up the stairs to the street.

Eleven

Alena waited. She stirred in terror in case the porridge burned, or Miss Calvert came back. 'How *dare* she talk to Tracey like that!' Alena muttered as she wrenched the sticky mess from side to side in the steaming pot.

She would have to leave soon. If she was late for school Mr Burns would strike her with the ruler.

At that moment, Tracey burst into the kitchen – her face radiant with joy. She dashed across the floor and hugged Alena, spoon and all.

'I got a call back!' she screamed.

Alena shook her head. What was she talking about?

'*A call back*!' Tracey shrieked again. 'They want me to come back and audition for a part. A singing *and* speaking part! O, my lord, I'm going to burst, I'm so happy.' She ripped off her apron and flung it into the air.

'No more porridge, my pet – come on! Let's go and celebrate with a real breakfast at the diner. And then I'm going to go and buy a beautiful dress at Macy's. I just have time before the call back at 11:30.'

'Wait,' Alena said. 'What are you going to use for money? Shouldn't you wait until you get the part?'

'I'm going to get the part,' Tracey stopped dancing around the kitchen and looked at Alena with shining eyes. 'The wish on the mummy's claw is working.'

Alena gave a sudden shudder. Tracey had left the door to the flight of steps leading up to the street open, and a blast of cold October air blew shrivelled autumn leaves down into the warm kitchen.

'It might not have been the c-claw,' she stammered. 'They might have called you back, anyway.'

'That's what they said!' Tracey cried. 'The show's director happened to be in the theatre when I walked on stage yesterday. They didn't want me in the chorus, but the director thinks I can play the part of a starving young actress. Can I!' She threw up her arms. 'Oh, Alena, I know it's going to work out this time. I can feel it in my bones.'

Alena felt swept up in Tracey's joy – at the same time as fear niggled at the back of her mind. 'I should go to school,' she hesitated. 'Miss Calvert . . .'

'As of this *second* we stop being afraid of Victoria Calvert!' Tracey crowed. 'Let her rant and rave and threaten! We won't care. Come on, I'm starving.'

Alena went with Tracey to the diner for breakfast, and then to shop at Macy's. Her friend, Marion, let her take the dress home 'on approval'.

'It's all right,' Tracey told Alena, 'the theatre always pays you an advance. I'll come back and pay for the dress when I get the cash. Isn't it perfect?' She twirled around in the fitting room.

The dress was perfect. It fitted Tracey's slim figure like a glove and made her look wistful and romantic.

The Majestic Theatre was on 44th Street. 'Well,' Tracey told Alena at the backstage door. 'Here goes.'

'Break a leg,' Alena cried. She crossed her fingers behind her back. What was happening to her? She was getting as superstitious as a theatre person. But it would be terrible

96

if Tracey were disappointed now, when her hopes were so high.

A kindly doorman let Alena wait backstage during Tracey's audition for the part of the starving actress. From the stage, Alena could hear the piano, and Tracey starting to sing. A chill shot down Alena's spine. She had never heard Tracey sing – never imagined such a beautiful voice.

There was muffled applause when she finished, then a long wait, and finally, Tracey appeared, her feet seeming not to touch the floor.

'I got it!' She hugged Alena tight. 'I start rehearsals tomorrow! Oh, Alena, this is it!'

Back at Haven House, Miss Calvert was pacing the floor, waiting for them, twisting the pearls at her neck in fury.

'What does this mean?' she screeched as they sailed through the front door. 'I had a call from your school, Alena. You weren't there all day! Tracey, get to the kitchen.' She shook her long, bony finger in Tracey's face.

'No, Miss Calvert, I will not get to the kitchen, now now, not ever!' Tracey said, grandly. 'Here is your fifty dollars, and another fifty for next month. But I'll be moving as soon as I find a new place.'

'Tracey has a part in a Broadway musical,' Alena burst out. 'A singing *and* speaking part.'

Miss Calvert took a step back.

She twisted her long strand of pearls nervously. 'Tracey, is this true?'

'At the Majestic,' Tracey said coolly. 'The show opens in three weeks.'

The next three weeks were a blur to Alena. Tracey rehearsed long hours, and when she came home, she wanted to tell Alena everything that had happened.

'It's just perfect,' she sighed one night. 'The director says I definitely have promise. The only problem is Ben.'

'Isn't he happy for you?' Alena asked. She was brushing Tracey's shining hair, and watching her friend's face in the mirror. It was true that she'd hardly heard Ben's cheerful whistle outside the window in the past weeks. Tracey was too tired to go out when she came home from rehearsal.

'Oh, of course he's thrilled for me. But he's running out of money too. Pretty soon he'll have to go back to the farm, and leave me here.'

'Couldn't he get a job in New York?'

Tracey laughed. 'There's not much work

for farmers in New York City.' Her face fell. 'I hope he can at least stay for the opening.'

Opening night was so exciting, Alena thought she would stop breathing. The seats at the Majestic were packed – women in long dresses and jewels, men in black tie and tails.

Alena sat in the third row. It seemed she had never seen anyone as lovely as Tracey, or heard a voice so pure and strong. When Tracey was on stage, singing, a strange hush fell over the audience, as though Tracey had spun a silver cord from her heart to each of theirs and they dared not move in case the cord was broken. When she stopped singing there was a pause of sheer wonderment before the thunderous applause burst from the crowd.

At the end, in the curtain calls, Tracey got more applause than anyone except the leading actors, and as she bowed, and smiled, Alena felt her joy spill over the footlights. Tracey blew a kiss in her direction, as she swept off the stage for the last time, and Alena sat, rapturous, listening to the comments of the people around her as they shuffled from their seats.

'What a beautiful voice . . .'

'Definitely, that girl is going to be a star . . .'

'Just think, we can say we saw her Broadway debut . . .'

Backstage, when Alena finally made her way through the crush, an eager crowd waited for Tracey to appear. Alena recognised Ben in his snap-brim hat and leather jacket, almost pushed to one side by the adoring fans.

A tall, distinguished-looking man in a tuxedo cruised through the crowd and rapped smartly on Tracey's dressing-room door.

'It's Emmett Barnes, the top director on Broadway,' Alena heard the whispers.

'Isn't she lucky he was in the audience,' someone else whispered.

The door opened, Emmett Barnes swept into Tracey's dressing room, and the door closed briskly again. 'Poor Ben,' Alena said to herself, looking at his woeful face. 'He can't get in, but a stranger named Barnes just waltzes through the door.'

A few minutes later, a flushed and smiling Tracey appeared on the arm of Emmett Barnes, dressed for the after-theatre party in a long, sparkling, evening gown.

'I'd like to announce,' Mr Barnes said

in his rich New York accent, 'that I have just signed Miss Tracey Winters for the lead in my new musical, *Chandelier*. Ladies and gentlemen, a new star has been born tonight.' He patted Tracey's hand with his own white-gloved one.

The waiting throng burst into applause. Tracey bowed and then Alena saw her eyes searching for Ben. 'Oh, there you are!' she cried, breaking away from Emmett Barnes and rushing to Ben's side. 'Did you like it, Ben?'

'It was fine,' Ben stammered, hating to be the centre of attention. 'But, I've heard you before, so I knew how good you could sing.'

The others burst into laughter, and Ben turned bright red. 'How charming,' Emmett Barnes said, 'Tracey tells me you're something of a handyman, and need a job. How would stage hand suit you?'

'Is it anything like a farm hand?' Ben said, blushing again.

The group around the stage door laughed heartily.

Tracey looked angry. 'Come on, Ben,' she took his arm. 'We're going to a party. We can talk about your job tomorrow.' She held out her hand to Alena. 'You come, too, darling,' she said. 'I want all the people I love around me.'

'Charming,' Emmett Barnes beamed again.

The next morning, Miss Calvert fluttered into the dining room, clutching the morning paper.

'Our Tracey is a star!' she crowed. 'It's all here in the papers – "a triumphant first performance" says *The New York Times*.' She stabbed at the review with a scarlet fingernail.

'Of course, we always *knew* she had great potential! And I am *proud* that Haven House has been a home and support while Tracey got her start, as it has been for so many other young women.'

Alena gaped at her. How dare old Calvert take credit for Tracey when she had tried to starve her and work her like a slave!

Now Miss Calvert could not do enough for Tracey. She insisted that she have a better room, on the second floor, with a private bath. She hoped Tracey would stay with them for a long, long time.

'I'm only staying because of you,' Tracey told Alena, as she folded her clothes to pack them for the move downstairs. 'Believe me, when I leave Haven House, you're coming with me!'

'Do you think I could?' Alena looked quickly at her friend.

'I've already insisted you have a room next-door to mine,' Tracey nodded. 'And when Ben and I are married, we could formally adopt you.'

Alena lay back on the bed, visions of her new life stretching before her. Ben was enjoying his stage hand job. He was the only one strong enough to lift the huge crystal chandelier above the centre of the stage. Alena could tell that Tracey felt safe and comfortable when he was backstage, and they planned to get married right after the opening night of *Chandelier*.

They would travel, all over the world, Alena thought. She could be Tracey's personal assistant, Ben would be a stage manager, Tracey would star in one triumph after another . . .

'You should get some sleep now,' Tracey said kindly. 'These late nights, keeping me company after rehearsal, are wearing you out. You look tired.'

'You're not my mother yet,' Alena smiled.

'I never *want* to be your mother!' Tracey cried. 'Just your sister and your friend. The adoption will only be paperwork, to get you away from Victoria Calvert.' Tracey shook her head. 'I don't think she'll let you go without a struggle.'

That night, as she left Tracey's room, Alena saw, once more, the strange glow in the dark hall leading to the stairs. She stood still, her spine prickling. A luminous shape wavered in the darkness. For a moment, Alena thought she saw the dead maid, Polly, crouched near the floor, sweeping dust from a corner into a dustpan. Alena rubbed her eyes, and the shape dissolved into Miss Calvert's glowing silk gown, sweeping down the hall towards her.

'There you are,' she said in a low, menacing voice. 'I suppose you've heard about your new room, next to Tracey Winters?'

'Y-yes,' Alena stammered. She was still shaking with terror at what she thought she had seen.

'I would have moved you in any case.' Miss Calvert said. 'Your funds have finally been cleared through the bank.'

Alena doubted Miss Calvert would have changed her room, but she said nothing.

'But don't think . . .' – Miss Calvert came closer, thrusting her beaked nose towards Alena's face – 'that you are going to leave here with Tracey. You are my ward, I am your official guardian, and *I*, not Tracey Winters, make decisions for you.'

She was listening! Alena thought with fury. Somehow she had heard everything they had said in Tracey's room. Alena was so angry she was speechless.

'Don't imagine,' Miss Calvert hissed, her hooded eyes unblinking, 'that I will *ever* let you go.'

'What a witch!' Charlie announced. 'Could she do that? I mean, legally?'

'I suppose some court, somewhere, had made her Alena's legal guardian,' Jo said. 'Mr Butterworth was too far away to do anything, so Miss Calvert had the same power as a parent.'

'That's terrible,' Alex said. 'Alena is almost grown up.'

'Well, *we're* grown up, and *we* still have to do what our parents say,' Jo pointed out.

'*And* our teachers,' Alex groaned.

'Sometimes,' Charlie laughed. 'Anyone want to go down to the hotel store again?'

'What for *this* time?' Jo asked. 'I'm full of chocolate mousse, pop and junk food. What now, Charlie?'

'This isn't food,' Charlie said. 'There's

something I saw in the store I want to get. If nobody wants to come, I'll go by myself.'

'There's no use arguing with her when she gets like this,' Louise sighed. 'We might as well go to the store with her.'

'But just a quick trip,' Jo complained. 'I want to hear the rest of Alena's story. There are still two wishes left on the mummy's claw!'

Twelve

'Hair dye!' Alex's eyebrows shot up. 'Charlie, what are you going to do with that?'

'I'm sick of my hair,' Charlie said, pulling her shining black hair into two wings on either side of her face. 'I think it would look better with highlights.'

'You mean blonde streaks,' Jo said. 'All this talk about looking glamorous is getting to you. Your hair is great the way it is.'

'But it's always the same,' Charlie tipped her head from one side to the other. 'Straight, and black.'

'That's right,' Alex moaned. 'It always looks great. Not like this mop . . .' She threw back her mass of reddish blonde curls.

'Are you really going to do it?' Louise asked, taking the packet out of Charlie's hand.

'Not now,' Charlie said. 'I want to hear the end of the story.'

'Are you sure?' Louise said. She gave a shiver and her voice sank. 'Why don't we dye your hair, instead?'

'Come on, Louise. What happened when Tracey got to star in a show? And did Alena manage to get away from Haven House?' Alex insisted.

'And why are you so afraid to tell us the rest?' Jo asked.

Louise flopped on the bed on her stomach, her chin in her hands. 'All right, guys, you asked for it!'

The others gathered around Louise on the bed. They watched Louise's eyes grow large and round as she reached back in her memory for details of the story and began to speak.

The new musical, *Chandelier*, opened at the Victory Theatre, on Broadway, in November. Alena rode with Tracey in a taxi to the theatre for the opening night performance.

Tracey clutched Alena's arm with both gloved hands. 'I'm so nervous,' she quavered. 'What if I can't sing? What if I open my mouth and all that comes out is a squawk?'

'You'll be fine,' Alena soothed.

'You're right,' Tracey recovered her dazzling smile. 'The mummy's claw will see that everything works out.'

Alena felt a chill, at the mention of the claw, and cranked the window of the taxi shut to keep out the cold night air.

'Alena, look! There's my name, in lights, just as I've always dreamed!'

The brilliant theatre marquee read clearly: STARRING TRACEY WINTERS. In the glaring lights of Broadway, Alena could see tears of joy trickle down Tracey's cheeks as they drew up in front of the theatre. Alena wished Tracey had not mentioned the wish on the mummy's claw. All this would be happening without any stupid wish. She was sure of that!

People pressed forward to touch Tracey's black velvet evening cape, and flashbulbs popped as she walked towards the Victory's doors.

And this time, the audience was not surprised at Tracey's beauty, charm and wonderful voice on stage. They applauded from the first moment she appeared and leaned forward eagerly when she began to sing.

Chandelier was the story of a princess who has been kidnapped and lost her memory.

All she can recall is the dazzling light of the huge crystal chandelier that hung in the palace ballroom when she was a child.

At the end of the play, when her true love has helped her regain her lost kingdom, the chandelier hangs once more over the ballroom as the lovers waltz below.

It was fabulous. Alena gasped and cheered along with the others, even though she knew the story backwards and forwards.

Finally, the curtains closed. The show was over, but the applause rang on and on. The actors ran on stage for curtain call after curtain call. Then there was one last call for the star, for Tracey. The curtains swept back a final time and there she stood, clutching scarlet roses to her white gown, all alone in the centre of the stage as the audience rose to their feet, cheering, whistling, clapping until their hands were red.

Suddenly, without warning, in the midst of the cheers and applause, it happened.

The crystal chandelier was falling. It hung by a shred of rope at a crazy angle, right over Tracey's head. In the same second, Alena saw a dark blur as a figure rushed from backstage and dived at Tracey, throwing her forward, and out of danger.

Then, there was an immense shattering

crash, as the chandelier, with its thousands of sharp crystals, smashed to the stage floor.

The audience, still on its feet, screamed with one voice.

The curtains swept shut, but not before Alena glimpsed blood, spattered on the shiny crystal, oozing across the wooden floor.

Then, above all the other screams and shouts, from behind the curtain, came a scream of such grief, such horror, that Alena buried her face in her hands.

'Ben! Oh, no! Not my Ben!'

Alena tried to block out the sound. Behind her closed eyes she saw again and again the image of the chandelier, plummeting towards the stage, and above it, a hovering pair of falcon's wings that only she could see . . .

The next morning, the New York City newspapers were full of the story.

'EXTRA, EXTRA, READ ALL ABOUT IT,' shouted the newsboys on every corner, 'BROADWAY STAR SAVED. LOVER CUT TO SHREDS BY FALLING CRYSTAL.'

Tracey's bedroom at Haven House was full of flowers. Alena moved them out to the hall. Red roses, she thought, would be the last thing Tracey would want to see when she opened her eyes. She lay in the middle of an enormous bed under a white satin bedspread.

The doctor had given her a powerful sedative, but still Tracey tossed in her sleep and called out for Ben.

Emmett Barnes, the director, came to see Tracey and left shaking his head. *Chandelier* was closed down, until further notice. He ordered the doctor to give Tracey the best of care and told him to send the bills to the theatre.

'I can't understand it,' Emmett told Alena. 'That chandelier rope was checked before every show.'

Alena sat beside Tracey's bed, sunk in terror and despair. All this – the luxurious room, Tracey's name in the papers, was for nothing. And no one except her knew the real reason the chandelier had fallen. The mummy's claw had struck again. It had waited until Tracey's triumphant moment to deliver the cruel twist to her wish come true.

An hour later, Tracey opened her slate blue eyes and gazed blankly around the room. 'Where's Ben?' she asked, in a child-ish voice. 'Alena? Is that you?' Her eyes fixed on Alena's face. 'What's the matter? Why are you crying?'

Then, suddenly, a look of horror swept over Tracey's face as she remembered. 'No!' she screamed. The colour fled from her face and her hands fell limply to her side.

The doctor hurried in at her cry. He frowned when he saw she had slipped back into unconsciousness. 'It's a kind of deep sleep,' he explained. 'She can't bear to think of what happened, so she slips away.' He shook his head. 'I don't like this.'

'What can we do?' Alena asked, wringing her hands.

'Keep her quiet,' the doctor said. 'And for heaven's sake, don't let any of those reporters or photographers in here. They'd be enough to throw her into a coma!'

The street outside Haven House was thronged with people from the newspapers, eager for a story. Miss Calvert encouraged them with hourly bulletins.

'She was always one of my favourite girls,' Alena heard Miss Calvert pronounce to a crowd of reporters in the front hall. 'We

113

knew she was a major talent. And of course, dear Ben . . . they were going to be married, you know. Right here, at Haven House, the home she loved.'

Miss Calvert struck a dramatic pose for the photographers, and flashbulbs popped.

Alena, on her way out for a breath of air, thought she would be sick. She would not put it past that woman to let the photographers take pictures of Tracey in her bed, or let the reporters pester her with questions. If only people knew the truth about Miss Calvert!

'Grab that girl,' she suddenly heard one of the reporters cry. 'I saw her get out of the cab with Tracey Winters at the theatre last night.'

Rough hands thrust Alena forward, into the circle of eager peering faces and camera lenses.

'What can you tell us about her condition?'

'Is her heart broken?'

'Will she ever act again?'

The questions flew like hot pepper, stinging her eyes.

'I . . . I can't tell you anything,' Alena stammered. 'She's still unconscious.'

'Did you hear that?' one of the reporters

cried. 'Still unconscious! New Broadway sensation may not recover!'

'What a story! Get some pictures of that kid.' More flashbulbs went off in Alena's eyes, and the mob of reporters pressed forward.

'What's your name, kid?'

'How long have you known Tracey Winters?'

Miss Calvert smoothly inserted herself between Alena and the cameras. 'This is Alena Sanger, another of my Haven House girls.' She tossed a cruel look back at Alena. When she spoke her words were dripping with meaning. 'Alena has had a lot to do with Tracey's success. I think you could say she has helped her *wish come true*.'

Alena felt her knees crumple. Did Miss Calvert know about the wish on the mummy's claw?

Thirteen

Miss Calvert's bony hand clutched Alena's arm, supporting her as she stood, swaying. 'The dear child's had a dreadful shock,' Alena heard Miss Calvert tell the reporters. 'You'll have to interview her later.'

The reporters buzzed off like a swarm of bees, racing to telephones to send in their stories. Miss Calvert, still gripping Alena's arm, led her back inside and to the elevator. 'You *must* get some rest,' she said with fake kindness. 'I will see you to your room.'

But on the way back to Alena's room, they met the doctor. 'Tracey's calling for you,' he told Alena. 'She insists on seeing you alone.'

Miss Calvert's eyes flashed. 'Is that really necessary, Doctor?'

'I'm afraid so,' the doctor nodded. 'Miss Winters is gravely ill. It is most important to keep her calm.'

'Very well,' Miss Calvert's eyes flashed a warning at Alena. 'Don't stay too long.' She walked away quickly down the hall.

With shaking hands, Alena turned the knob of the bedroom door.

'Alena? Is that you?' she heard Tracey whisper as she opened the door. The room was darkened. Tracey was sitting up, propped against the satin pillows. Her fine soft hair surrounded her face. Her blue eyes looked strangely happy.

'Open the window! I hear Ben, whistling for me. He's outside, on the street.' Her voice was as excited as a happy child.

Alena crossed the room and opened the blinds. She looked out at the dreary, windswept November street. It was still early, but already the street lights were on. Alena saw wet leaves plastered in the wet gutters, bare trees and narrow lamp-posts. That was all.

'He's not there,' Alena said.

'But can't you hear him whistling? It's *Yankee Doodle*.'

'No, I can't hear him,' Alena said.

There was a long silence. Alena stood by the window. Then Tracey spoke, in her normal voice.

'He's not coming, is he?'

'No,' Alena said, leaning her forehead against the glass.

'Come here, and tell me what happened,' Tracey said. 'I can't – I can't remember. No one will tell me the truth.'

Alena went over and sat on the bed. She took Tracey's pale hand in her own.

'You were wonderful on stage last night,' she said. 'And Ben saved your life. He was a hero, Tracey.'

'Something . . . fell . . .' Tracey looked frightened.

'He saw the chandelier falling on you,' Alena nodded. 'He shoved you out of the way . . .'

Tracey rolled her head from side to side, her eyes squeezed tightly shut. 'Now I remember – It's all my fault! I should never have got Ben that job. He didn't really want to work in the theatre – he loved his farm, being outside in the wide open spaces . . .'

Her voice rose. 'If I hadn't been so blind, so selfish, he would be alive now! I didn't think about him. All I thought about was *myself*. I will never act again. Never set foot on a stage as long as I live! I want him back – I can't go on without him!'

'It was my fault, too,' Alena said. 'If

I hadn't wished on the mummy's claw, maybe none of this would have happened.'

At that moment Tracey's door burst open and Victoria Calvert stood in the frame of light from the hall.

'I thought so,' she cried in triumph. 'You little, no talent, country girl. How could *you* become a Broadway star without a secret power pushing you forward!'

Alena got shakily to her feet. 'You've been spying on us,' she said. 'But you don't know what you're talking about!'

'Don't I? I know you wished on an old bird's foot that you brought with you from Egypt,' Victoria Calvert cried. Her feathery shawl rustled around her as she strode to the bed. 'I found it in your luggage the first week you were here. *I want you to tell me how it works.*'

Alena was about to protest when she felt Tracey's hand tighten on her own. She glanced down at her friend. Tracey's eyes were on fire with an unhealthy light.

'Only the owner can wish on the claw,' Tracey whispered. 'Alena can't give it to you, yet. She still has two wishes left.'

Miss Calvert glared down her beak-like nose at Alena.

'Is this true?'

'Yes . . .' Alena stammered, feeling Tracey's iron grip on her hand.

'Well, hurry and use them then,' Miss Calvert suggested. 'But don't try to get away from me. I mean to have that power for myself.'

She swished from the room, her shawl flowing behind her, and slammed the door.

Alena was afraid to look at Tracey, afraid of that fierce light in her eyes.

'Alena!' she heard Tracey gasp. 'We forgot about the other wishes.'

'You can forget the whole thing,' Alena blurted. 'Hasn't that horrible claw done enough damage? That falling chandelier was meant for you, Tracey. I saw it. If it hadn't been for Ben, you would have been killed!'

'And if it hadn't been for me, he would be alive now. I'd rather be his wife in Wisconsin for the rest of my life than never see him again!'

'Please,' Alena begged. 'Please rest, Tracey.' She was terrified of Tracey's excitement.

'But, don't you see? You can use the second wish to bring him back to me,' Tracey clutched at her arm. 'I want him back, Alena. Wish that he was alive. Wish on the mummy's claw.'

'Bring him back to life? Tracey, that's not possible. He . . .' Alena shut her eyes, thinking of the way she had seen Ben's shattered body in that moment before the theatre curtain had swept shut.

'I don't care!' Tracey's voice rose to a wail. 'Bring him back. I just want him *back*.' She twisted in the bed, gripping Alena's arm so hard it hurt.

'I'm going for the doctor,' Alena pulled away.

By the time Alena had found the doctor, Tracey had lapsed into a feverish dream. The doctor shook his head. 'She's wearing herself out,' he said. 'When was the last time she ate or drank anything?'

Alena rubbed her tired forehead. Time had become so twisted it was hard to remember what day it was, or how long it had been since that terrible moment at the theatre. 'Yesterday . . . sometime,' she finally said. 'Tracey didn't want to eat before her performance.'

'Ridiculous,' the doctor said severely. 'She must be made to take some nourishment.'

Alena sat with Tracey through an anxious

night and all the next day. Tracey refused to eat or drink. She woke from her feverish dreams every few hours, then she would lapse back into unconsciousness or sleep. Alena dozed in a chair at these times and woke when Tracey tossed and turned and called Ben's name.

It was almost midnight when the doctor made his final call. 'Her pulse is very uneven,' the doctor frowned when he held Tracey's limp wrist between his fingers. 'Her heart won't stand much more of this.'

He looked sternly at Alena, sitting rigidly by the bedside. 'There is something she wants from you,' he said. 'She keeps begging you to help her. If it is in your power to do so, I suggest that you waste no time.'

'Do you think she might die?' Alena asked, alarmed by the doctor's serious face.

Again he shook his head. 'She is the most intense young woman I have ever treated,' he said. 'She has made herself quite ill with grief. What does she want when she begs you to help?'

'She thinks I can bring Ben back to life,' Alena said.

The doctor patted Alena's hand. 'Poor child,' he said. 'Then there is no way you can help her. Her mind is beyond our reach.

Try to get some rest yourself, and if you can, try to get her to take a little water. I will be back in the morning.'

The doctor left the room. Alena heard the elevator creak down to the ground floor. She sat, trembling, thinking of his parting words. He imagined Tracey was crazy. He knew nothing about the mummy's claw, and why she begged Alena to help!

Alena looked at Tracey's pale, exhausted face. 'She will die,' Alena whispered to herself. 'She means it when she says she doesn't want to live without Ben.'

Alena stood up. She was so stiff and tired from sitting, she could hardly walk, but she staggered across the bedroom floor. She locked Tracey's door from the inside. The claw was hidden in a place where not even Miss Calvert or her spies could find it, but she was taking no chances.

Perhaps Tracey's stardom had come by her own talent and hard work. Maybe Ben's death was an accident. There *were* still logical explanations for everything that had happened, Alena thought. And, maybe, if she wished on the claw, and Ben didn't come back, Tracey would accept his death and get well. It was worth a try!

With a surge of hope, Alena crossed to

Tracey's bed and smoothed the tangled hair back from her friend's forehead.

'All right,' she murmured. 'All right, I will wish that Ben comes back to life. Can you hear me, Tracey? I'm going to use the second wish.'

She had to repeat it many times, but at last Tracey's eyes opened, and she tried to speak.

'Th-thank you, Alena.'

'First,' Alena said, 'you must just take a little sip of water. I need you to be awake, to help me with the wish.'

Tracey obediently sipped from the glass Alena held to her lips. 'That's good,' Alena told her. 'One or two more sips, and we'll be ready.'

Tracey shook her head, but managed to drink a little more. Alena watched her eyes begin to focus on the room around her.

'Oh, quick, Alena. Make the wish.'

'Wait,' Alena told her, 'I have to get the claw. I hid it so Miss Calvert couldn't find it.'

She crossed the room to Tracey's dressing table. It was an oval table with a frilled skirt hanging to the floor. Alena sat on a low stool in front of the mirror and gazed at the array of jars and bottles on the table. Her reflection looked unreal in the dim light. Dark circles were etched under her eyes from lack of sleep. 'I hope I'm doing the right thing,' she muttered.

She had hidden the mummy's claw in a round box of face powder. As she dug her fingers into the soft powder she felt the hated hard scaliness of the claw. She forced herself to lift it gently, blowing the loose powder from its talons.

It looked even more evil now that it was powdered white – a ghostly, glowing thing. Alena placed it in her left palm and carried it to the bed.

'I'm ready, Tracey,' she said shakily.

'Ben,' Tracey gasped. 'Tell him to come quickly. I want to tell him how sorry I am – how wrong I was . . .'

Alena looked down at the wrinkled thing on her palm. 'I wish,' she gasped, 'I wish on the ancient claw of Horus the sun god that Ben Hinckley comes back . . .'

'Comes back to life,' Tracey whispered. 'I want him alive.'

'Comes back to life,' Alena shuddered. Her head swam. Did the claw really dig into her palm once more? As if it were some horrible, live creature, she dropped it on the floor and raised her foot to stomp it into dust.

'Listen,' Tracey grabbed her hand, throwing her off balance. 'Do you hear anything?'

Alena listened. The old hotel was making its usual night noises – creaks and bangs in the wall. There was a swish of traffic on the street outside.

'Can't you hear that?' Tracey cried. 'It sounds like someone humming. Maybe it's him, Alena. Go to the door and see.'

Alena heard nothing, but Tracey's face was so wild with hope that she went to the door, turned the lock, and slowly opened the door.

There was no one there.

'There's no one in the hall, Tracey,' Alena said, feeling an enormous relief.

Then she saw the black cat, its back arched, hissing and spitting at a greenish-blue light, close to the floor. The light pulsed and throbbed, getting stronger, becoming a shape.

'Are you sure?' Tracey called behind her. 'Are you sure Ben's not there?'

'No-o,' Alena managed to choke. 'Ben is not here.'

But Polly was.

Polly, the ghost of an orphan maid, with

her apron and white cap. Alena could see her clearly. Polly was waving her arms as though distressed. Her face was a grimace of pain, screaming, 'No! No!' over and over without making a sound.

'She's warning us,' Alena whispered in terror. 'She's warning us that something horrible is happening.'

THUMP, THUMP, THUMP!

'Holy mackerel,' Jo dived under a bedspread, 'It's Ben!'

'Jesse . . . and Mark,' Charlie cried.

'Mr Makepeace!' Alex hissed. 'Turn out the lights!'

'Are you *kidding*,' Jo said. 'If you turn out the lights now, my teeth are going to rattle right out of my head!'

'I w-warned you,' Louise shivered.

THUMP, THUMP – 'It's Room Service. Are you finished with the cart?' came a voice from the hall.

'Oh, phew,' Jo poked her head out from the bedspread. 'It's just that cute bellboy. He wants his cart.'

'Wait a minute,' Charlie said, jumping up. 'How do we *know* it's the bellboy?'

The others nodded. 'It's getting late,' Louise said. 'Maybe we shouldn't open the door.'

'We're all asleep,' Alex shouted. 'Come back in the morning.'

'Okay,' came the cheerful response. 'Just shove the cart into the hall when you're finished with it. Goodnight.'

They heard footsteps and whistling disappearing down the hall.

'I guess it really *was* the bellboy,' Jo said.

'This story is really getting to us,' Alex put her hand over her heart. 'I nearly jumped out of my skin when I heard that knock . . . what's going to happen, Louise?'

Fourteen

'Just imagine . . .' Alex was standing at the window, looking out at the city. 'It all happened right here. Alena could have been looking out of a window, just like this, waiting for Ben to come back.'

She turned and walked slowly across the room, looking down at Louise. 'I have a feeling . . .' she said. 'Nothing good's going to come out of this wish, right, Louise?'

She slumped down with the rest of them, cross-legged in her favourite sitting position. 'Okay, I'm ready.'

Louise scanned her friends' faces in the pale lamplight. Charlie with her bright brown eyes, Jo with her chin in her hands, Alex with her curls tumbling around her face. They were all waiting.

Louise took a deep, shuddering breath and began to speak.

* * *

129

Alena waited with a sense of sickening dread. Tracey had fallen into a restless sleep. It was very late – even the scurrying taxis had deserted the street. A slow, steady rain was falling and the reporters had given up their watch by the front door.

Once Tracey woke to murmur, 'Why don't you go down to the front lobby and see if Ben is waiting?' She sighed. 'You know Miss Calvert wouldn't let him come upstairs.'

'Miss Calvert is in bed,' Alena shivered. She was afraid to venture out in the hall again in case the ghost of Polly was still there. When she shut her eyes, the image of Polly's screaming face returned. 'I'm so tired,' Alena told herself. 'Maybe I'm just seeing things.'

She collapsed in the chair beside Tracey's bed, fighting back the waves of sleep. A sudden, clear whistle made her sit bolt upright. Gripping the arms of the chair, Tracey stared over her shoulder at the window. Someone was whistling, out on the street.

Tracey was pulling at her sleeve. Her face was transformed with joy. 'Can you hear him now, Alena?'

Alena could. The old tune of *Yankee Doodle*, slow, and unbearably sad, floated up through the open window.

Alena sat frozen in her chair. 'Let it be a policeman, on the beat,' she prayed. 'Let him pass by.'

But the whistler halted outside Haven House. The whistling continued. There was a pause, then the sound of shuffling foot-steps, coming up the stone steps. 'Let the door be locked,' Alena prayed. Miss Calvert was always very particular about locking the door.

Her grip tightened on the arms of the chair. Did she hear the faint creak of the large front door?

Tracey's grey-blue eyes were shining with excitement. 'Ben!' she whispered. 'He's coming.'

Yes, he was coming. There was no doubt now. The elevator creaked upwards. The elevator cage door banged open, echoing down the empty hall.

The low sad whistle came again.

Alena leaned forward, her eyes staring, her heart thudding, waiting . . . for footsteps in the hall. When at last they came, she shook with fear. The footsteps were drag-ging, slow, not at all like Ben's brisk walk.

'Run to the door,' Tracey raised her head from the pillow. 'Let him in.'

Alena moved as though she were a puppet

131

on a string. Against her will, against every fibre of her being, she rose to her feet as the shuffling footsteps came closer.

'Go!' Tracey whispered.

Alena felt as though her legs must buckle under her. She wanted to run, to hide, to do anything but go to that door.

Still, Tracey's desire propelled her forward.

The footsteps stopped again. There was another long silence. Alena froze in the middle of the floor.

'Ben,' Tracey called from the bed behind her. 'Is that you, Ben?'

A muffled knock came at the door.

Alena reached for the handle. She wrenched open the door. Her mouth opened in a soundless scream. The *thing* that stood there was not the living Ben. Its torn hands were raised in helpless pleading, its eyes were pools of pain in a hideously mangled face. With all her strength, Alena slammed the door shut.

Her ears registered Tracey's wail of despair. 'No, Alena, don't shut him out!'

The muffled knocks continued. Thump. Thump. Thump.

Suddenly, Alena knew what she had to do. She couldn't let Tracey see him! She ran to the bed, scrabbling underneath it, feeling for the claw. At last her hand closed on the fearful thing and, breathless, sobbing, kneeling beside Tracey with the claw in her hand, Alena wished her final wish.

'By the power of the claw of Horus the sun god, I wish Ben Hinckley back in his grave!' she screamed.

'Oh, NO!' Tracey howled.

Alena gripped her friend's hand. 'Tracey. Listen to me. Listen!' Alena summoned all the fierceness of her heart. 'He was begging me. Begging me not to let you see him like that!'

Tracey could not hear. She had slipped back into unconsciousness.

Alena stood up, shaking with fury and terror, and flung the claw on the floor. 'It's done. It's over, and now I'm going to crush this evil thing to dust!'

She raised her foot over the claw.

'I wouldn't do that,' came a sudden voice.

Alena turned with a stifled gasp.

A section of Tracey's wall had swung open, and there stood Victoria Calvert in a jewelled green gown. Behind her was a dark cavity.

'Forgive my interruption,' she said. 'This secret staircase my father installed years ago leads to rooms we reserve for our very special guests.' She gestured to the opening behind her.

'But how foolish to destroy the mummy's claw,' Miss Calvert came forward. 'Why not use it?'

'Never again!' Alena cried. 'Look what it has done to my friend!' This time, she feared, Tracey might *never* wake up.

'I don't mean *you* should wish on it again,' Miss Calvert smiled cruelly. She crossed the room and gazed greedily down at the claw on the floor. 'I suggest that you hand the claw over to me. In return I will give you your freedom. I will suggest to Dr Butterworth that he appoint a new guardian for you.'

Alena met Miss Calvert's cold, blank eyes. She gulped. Miss Calvert was offering a chance to get away from Haven House. It was what she longed for. But she couldn't pass on the curse of the mummy's claw to another person, however much she hated her.

'No,' she said. She raised her foot and stomped on the claw with all her strength. It was as if the claw were made of steel. It skittered out from under her foot, undamaged.

'I won't give it to you!' Alena shouted. She bent over to pick up the claw.

But Victoria Calvert was faster. She thrust

Alena aside, swooped low and clutched the claw to her jewelled gown. 'Now, how does it work?' she demanded. 'Magic words? Turning circles three times?'

'I won't tell you,' Alena said.

Miss Calvert glared at her.

'I'll figure it out, don't worry,' Miss Calvert laughed. 'I'm a very determined woman. And with three wishes I can be a very rich, very happy woman. I have always wanted to fly, like a bird, across the ocean. Now, it will be possible, along with so many other things I've wanted.'

Alena tried one more time. 'You will be sorry if you wish on the claw. Please, let me destroy it,' she begged.

Miss Calvert ignored her. She looked down at Tracey with another cruel smile. 'Poor Tracey,' she said. 'Now that she doesn't have the power of the claw, I'm afraid she'll go right back to being what she was – a little nobody.'

Victoria Calvert turned and swept from the room, still clutching the claw in one hand. Her secret door swung silently shut, leaving barely any trace in the panelling.

Alena slumped on her knees by Tracey's bed, staining the satin bedspread with her tears. Tracey's hand remained limp in her own. The image of Ben's terrible wounded face was etched behind Alena's eyelids. At least she had saved Tracey that sight.

Or had she? Alena's head jerked up. She had heard whistling again . . . coming from the street!

Alena slowly rose from her kneeling position and stumbled to the window. She stared into the quiet night. There was a tall shadowy figure waiting by the lamp-post. Alena heard the door of Haven House open. It seemed to her that the light from the open door shone right through the waiting figure by the lamp-post.

Then another shape floated down the steps, surrounded by a pale, flickering blue light. She saw a flash of a white cap, a white apron. Alena clutched her heart. Polly's ghost!

The whistling stopped. The two ghostly figures met and merged. The whistling began again, clear and joyful, then faded as they floated away down the rainswept street.

'Ben . . . and Polly,' Alena breathed. 'He's taking her with him.'

She glanced back at the bed. Had Tracey heard the whistling?

But Tracey lay as still as before.

'Maybe it's just as well,' Alena whispered to the night. Someday, if Tracey got well, she would tell her what she'd seen.

For now, a feeling of such weariness swept over Alena that she collapsed in the chair and into a deep sleep.

There was silence in the hotel room as Louise stopped talking.

'That's not the end, is it?' Jo asked. 'What happened to Tracey?'

'And Miss Calvert!' Alex added. 'Did she figure out how to wish on the claw?'

'I think Alena could have dreamed the whole thing about Ben coming back as a corpse,' Charlie said. 'Or she might have been hallucinating because she was so tired.'

'Maybe,' Louise agreed. 'And maybe what happened to Miss Calvert later was just a coincidence . . .'

'What happened?' Jo cried.

'Tell us,' Alex echoed.

'Wait! Don't tell the rest yet,' Charlie jumped to her feet. 'First, I want to try this stuff on my hair.'

'Charlie, you're not really going to dye your hair!' Jo exclaimed.

'What will your mother say?' Louise asked.

'My mother says my hair belongs to me,' Charlie shrugged, 'And she doesn't care what I do with it.'

'Still,' Alex sighed. 'She's going to be awfully surprised if you come home from New York as a blonde.'

Fifteen

'It says on the box it's not permanent,' Charlie told them, coming out of the bathroom with her hair wound up in a towel. 'It will rinse out . . . in a few weeks.'

'Let's see what it looks like,' Jo tossed her own dark hair back.

'It's not done yet,' Charlie patted the towel. 'I have to keep it wrapped in the towel for a while, then wash it again,' Charlie flopped back down on their bed of mattresses. 'Louise has time to tell us the end of the story. Come on, Louise. What happened after Alena saw the ghosts of Ben and Polly?'

Louise took a long gulp of water and dived back into the story.

When Alena woke up it was morning, and the doctor was bending over Tracey.

Alena jumped up in alarm. Had he come too late . . . ?

139

'It's all right, my dear,' he said kindly. 'She's sleeping peacefully. She'll recover now – she's young.' He left, giving orders for food and liquids as soon as Tracey woke.

It was hours later when Tracey opened her eyes. 'I was dreaming of Ben,' she said. 'He was back on the farm . . .' her voice caught with a sob. 'I want to go home too. It was all such a foolish dream, wanting to be an actress . . . Ben always knew that.'

Alena clasped her friend's hand. 'Tracey, it wasn't a dream,' she said. 'And it wasn't magic, either. I saw you, and heard you. You were great, sensational! You *have* to go on. I *need* you.'

Tracey turned her sad eyes to Alena, and Alena rushed on, while the words were in her head. 'I never thought I needed anyone, but now I need you. I need you to be my friend. I need you to be strong, and help me get away from Miss Calvert. I need you to be a great star so you can take me with you. You can't give up and go back to Wisconsin! What will happen to me?'

Tracey gave her a puzzled frown. 'I didn't think . . . about you,' she mumbled.

'And it's not just me.' Alena rushed on. 'There are dozens of reporters downstairs. They think you're wonderful – the whole city thinks you're wonderful. They're waiting to hear whether you will go back on the stage.'

Tracey shuddered. 'The show!' she gasped. 'The chandelier . . . I couldn't . . .'

'There will be other shows,' Alena urged. 'Lots of them. Listen, don't just do it for me. When you sing . . . it's a gift to everyone who hears you.' She was stumbling over her words, trying to reach through the veil of pain surrounding Tracey.

She could see a spark of light in the eyes that searched her face. 'That's . . .' Tracey swallowed. 'That's how it felt up there . . . like I was giving something inside myself . . . something too big . . .'

Too big for Ben, or any one person, or the whole state of Wisconsin, Alena thought. She squeezed Tracey's hand. 'Let me get you a drink,' she said. 'You don't want to strain your voice.'

Alena was right. There were many other shows for Tracey. Within a week they had moved to a fabulous apartment on Park Avenue, and Tracey had signed a long-running contract with Emmett Barnes to star in his new musicals.

And from now on there was a Tracey Winters tradition at the end of each performance. For the last curtain call, Tracey would always turn her back to the audience. And standing centre stage, she would bow, and blow a kiss to someone only she could see. No matter how big a star she became, Tracey would never forget . . .

Alena stayed with her as her assistant until she finished school and went to university. There she studied animal behaviour, and became an expert on birds of prey – hawks, eagles and falcons.

Alena's prediction about Miss Calvert turned out to be true, too. At first it seemed she *would* get everything she wanted – including her flight across the ocean. Like I said . . . there were no long distance passenger flights back then. But there *were* hydrogen- and helium-filled airships that crossed the Atlantic. Some of them were huge, with sleeping quarters and dining lounges just like an ocean liner.

Miss Calvert flew on one of the airships to Europe. She went on a wild shopping spree in London, Paris and Rome. In May, 1937, she was flying back across the Atlantic on the *Hindenburg*, a luxury airship that carried 92 passengers. With her were trunks full of gowns, jewels, priceless art and . . . the claw.

The photograph is famous. Just as the *Hindenburg* was touching down at Lakehurst, New Jersey, it suddenly burst into flames. Alena and Tracey were listening to the radio when the tragic news came through. The radio reporter was in tears as he described the enormous airship, tipped on its end, burning . . .

Thirty-six people were killed, but Miss Calvert lived. That might have been her final wish . . . to survive the crash. Her badly burned body was dragged from the wreckage. The rescuers said she was delirious – muttering about her precious belongings being destroyed in the fire, and the claw playing a trick on her.

In the end she had to sell Haven House to pay her medical bills, and moved to a small apartment in a poor part of the city, where she lived alone until she died.

'But you couldn't blame Alena,' Charlie insisted. 'After all, she refused to give the claw to Miss Calvert.'

'Maybe it wasn't the claw's doing at all,' Alex mused. 'Just some good luck, and then some bad luck.'

'All the same,' Jo shivered, 'it's a relief to know the claw must have burned up in the crash. I can just picture it . . . a smouldering cinder in all that debris . . .'

'I don't think so,' said Louise in a shaky, low voice, 'I don't think the claw burned up . . . because HERE IT IS!' she suddenly screamed, tossing something into the centre of the group.

'The claw!' Charlie screeched, throwing herself backwards.

With gasps of horror, Jo and Alex shrank away from the brown shrivelled object on the white sheet.

'What . . . ?' Alex stuttered. 'What *is* this?'

'Louise?' Jo clutched her friend's arm.

Louise had buried her face in a pillow. When she lifted her head, they could see it was bright red.

'Got you!' she howled with laughter.

'It's just a dried-up old chicken foot,' Alex said in disgust, poking at it with one finger. 'Where did you get it?'

Louise was still laughing. 'I found it in the science supply cupboard at school, when we were looking for stuff to build our display,' She looked from one to another. 'Oh, if you could have seen your faces! . . . *The claw* . . .' She smothered her face in the pillow again.

'You brought that old chicken foot with you?' Jo shook her head. 'You've been planning this for days! You just *pretended* to be scared to tell us the story!'

'Well, you guys always have such excellent scary stories, and I knew it was my turn, so . . .' Louise chuckled.

'You got even,' Alex sighed. 'I would have expected it from Charlie, but not you, Louise.'

'What a great acting job!' Jo said. 'You had me totally convinced you were terrified.'

'Me, too.' Charlie admitted. Her towel turban had fallen off when she did her backward somersault away from 'the claw'. She leaned back into the circle of lamplight for a closer look at the chicken foot.

'Charlie!' Jo suddenly gasped. 'Your hair!'

145

Sixteen

'Don't worry, Charlie, the dye will wash out,' Jo soothed.

'It's orange!' Charlie gasped.

'I think it looks cool,' Alex said.

'But it's *orange*.' Charlie repeated numbly.

'It's different,' Louise soothed. 'Unique.'

'Can't you see . . . ?' Charlie shouted, 'my hair is orange!' It was true that Charlie's glossy black hair was streaked with pale, carroty orange. She stared at herself in horror in the mirror. 'I'm going to wash it again,' she cried, and ran for the shower.

'I didn't think it looked so bad,' Alex shrugged.

'Be careful what you wish for,' Jo shook her head. 'Isn't that what your great-uncle Taylor used to say, Louise?'

'Poor Charlie,' Louise said. 'She wanted Jesse to notice her. I think he'll notice.'

'Speaking of those two geniuses – we still have to get back at them for that robot fire hose trick,' Alex jumped up.

'They'll be expecting something,' Louise said. 'It will have to be good.'

'I have an idea,' Jo said. 'Let's call them up, and say that Mr Makepeace wants to have a meeting – he's got some fabulous idea for the contest tomorrow – Alex, you can pretend to be Mr Makepeace on the phone.'

'*Okay boys, we'll meet in ten minutes. You got that?*' Alex practised her imitation of Mr Makepeace.

'Perfect,' Jo laughed.

'And then what?' Louise said. 'We get them to a meeting and then . . .'

'We need Charlie's diabolical brain for this,' Jo said. 'Charlie, get out here.'

Charlie emerged from the bathroom, with her wet hair plastered to her skull. 'It doesn't look so bad, wet,' she said. 'I'll just go around for a few weeks with my hair greased down.' She fell on the bed, groaning.

'Never mind your hair. We need your brain,' Jo explained.

Charlie gave a wicked grin when she heard their plan for a late night meeting. 'This will be sensational!' she said.

Ten minutes later they crept down the hallway past the boys' door. They taped a sign to the elevator:

OUT OF ORDER
PLEASE USE THE STAIRS

with an arrow pointing to the old staircase.

'Now we need to dim the light somehow,' Jo said, pointing to the bare bulb in its wire cage. 'If we unscrew the bulb it will be too dark.'

'How about a thick towel over the whole thing,' Alex suggested.

The towel worked. The light was perfect. 'Now, you get things set up, while I go and telephone the guys,' Alex said. 'How long will it take you?'

'Tell them five minutes,' Jo said, rattling down the spiral metal stairs. 'Tell them to meet outside Mr Makepeace's door on the fourth floor. We'll get set up on the fourth floor landing.'

'I wonder what old Makepeace wants at this time of night,' they heard Jesse yawn as he pushed open the door to the stairwell.

'Wow, what weird old stairs!' That was Mark's voice. 'Do you think he meant these?'

'The sign on the elevator pointed in this direction,' Jesse answered. 'Come on. It's just one floor down.'

'Ready . . . ?' Jo whispered below.

'Any second,' Louise whispered back. 'Here it goes!'

The sound of popcorn popping in the narrow stairwell was magnified many times. It sounded like an explosion, like a machine gun – POP! POP! POPPOPPOPPOP! POP!

Jesse and Mark fled, scrambling back up the stairs – only to find themselves confronted by a glowing white shape at the top of the stairs.

'Ahhh-hh! He-elp!'

'Let me out of here!'

'HALT!' came a terrible voice that rose above the rapid fire popcorn explosions from below. 'You have stumbled into an alternate universe . . . THERE IS NO ESCAPE.'

'Jesse,' Mark screamed. 'Do you smell popcorn?'

The six of them sat on the stairs, munching hot popcorn.

'How did you do it?' Mark asked.

Alex juggled three popcorn kernels as she explained. 'I was the solar-powered ghost at the top of the stairs. It was easy – a bed sheet and some solar battery lights underneath.'

'And Louise, Charlie and I were the popping crew down below,' Jo said. 'We had this back-up popcorn maker with us in case something goes wrong with our display tomorrow.'

'I'd better get the towel off the light,' Alex said, throwing the last bit of popcorn into her mouth. 'We don't want to start a fire.' She bounded up the spiral stairs.

Just then, the door to the floor below swung open. A hotel security man in a blue uniform stood glaring at them. 'What are you kids doing in here?' he growled. 'The management has had some complaints about noise . . .'

'*I'll see that they get straight to bed*,' Mr Makepeace's firm voice floated down the stairwell. '*Don't worry, young man.*'

'Oh, no problem, sir. I didn't realise you were with the kids.' The security man backed politely out the door, letting it close behind him.

'Good work, Alex,' Jo burst into giggles. 'You sound exactly like him.'

'I'm glad,' Alex said, 'I wouldn't want old Makepeace to get into trouble because of us. He's really a nice guy – for a teacher!'

They clattered on up the metal stairs. Under the light, Jesse stopped in shock.

'Charlie,' he said. 'Something's happened to your hair!'

'I . . . uh . . . it's a new look,' Charlie stammered. 'Solar . . . uh . . . orange.'

Jesse shoved his glasses up his nose. 'I liked the *old* look!' he said.

Charlie gazed at him. 'You did?'

Jesse nodded. 'It was always so smooth, and shiny . . .' he said sadly.

Charlie flushed. 'This will wash out,' she said. 'It's no big deal.'

Jo, Louise and Alex exchanged glances. 'Be careful what you wish for . . .' they all said together.

On their way home the following afternoon, the sleepover gang turned for a last view of the Manhattan skyline as they sped over the bridge across the Hudson River.

The back of Mr Makepeace's van was crowded with their luggage, equipment, and two large trophies.

'I guess we showed them we're not hicks from Lakeview,' Mark sighed with satisfaction. 'Second prize for you four, and honourable mention for Jesse and me.'

Jo yawned. 'I can't wait to get home.'

'Going to show off your trophy?' Mr Makepeace beamed.

'No,' Jo yawned. 'I'm going to sleep for about two days.'

They settled down for the long drive to Lakeview, their heads on their rucksacks, the yawns spreading from one to the other.

'It's been a big day,' Mr Makepeace glanced at them in his rearview mirror. 'I guess all the excitement at the Science Fair wore you out.'

Behind him, the sleepover gang winked at each other, then closed their eyes . . .

THE SECRET ROOM SLEEPOVER

Sharon Siamon

Dark shadows give Jo the jitters . . .

Settled in the candlelit cellar of Jo's old house, the Sleepover gang munch snacks and snuggle down to listen. Jo has a very strange story to tell. Will it scare easy-going Alex, frighten timid Louise or chill Charlie, the junk-food queen? It's time to find out . . .

THE CAMP-FIRE SLEEPOVER

Sharon Siamon

The smell of smoke sets off Charlie's story . . .

Crouched round a crackling camp-fire, the Sleepover gang fan the flames and get ready to listen. Charlie has a spooky story to tell. Will it stir Jo from her troubles, transfix fun-loving Alex or give Louise uneasy shivers? It's time to find out . . .

ORDER FORM

THE SLEEPOVER SERIES
Sharon Siamon

0 340 67276 5	THE SECRET ROOM SLEEPOVER	£3.99	☐
0 340 67277 3	THE SNOWED-IN SLEEPOVER	£3.99	☐
0 340 67278 1	THE HAUNTED HOTEL SLEEPOVER	£3.99	☐
0 340 67279 X	THE CAMP FIRE SLEEPOVER	£3.99	☐
0 340 70904 9	THE SHIVERING SEA SLEEPOVER	£3.99	☐

All Hodder Children's books are available at your local bookshop or newsagent, or can be ordered direct from the publisher. Just tick the titles you want and fill in the form below. Prices and availability subject to change without notice.

Hodder Children's Books, Cash Sales Department, Bookpoint, 39 Milton Park, Abingdon, OXON, OX14 4TD, UK. If you have a credit card, our call centre team would be delighted to take your order by telephone. Our direct line is *01235 400414* (lines open 9.00 am – 6.00 pm Monday to Saturday, 24 hour message answering service). Alternatively you can send a fax on *01235 400454*.

Or please enclose a cheque or postal order made payable to Bookpoint Ltd to the value of the cover price and allow the following for postage and packing:
UK & BFPO – £1.00 for the first book, 50p for the second book, and 30p for each additional book ordered up to a maximum charge of £3.00.
OVERSEAS & EIRE – £2.00 for the first book, £1.00 for the second book, and 50p for each additional book.

Name ....

Address ....

....

....

If you would prefer to pay by credit card, please complete:
Please debit my Visa/Access/Diner's Card/American Express (delete as applicable) card no:

☐☐☐☐☐ ☐☐☐☐☐ ☐☐☐☐☐ ☐☐☐☐☐

Signature ....

Expiry Date ....